DOWN AMONG THE
STICKS AND BONES

Center Point
Large Print

Also by Seanan McGuire and available from Center Point Large Print:

Every Heart a Doorway

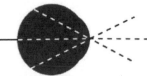

This Large Print Book carries the Seal of Approval of N.A.V.H.

DOWN AMONG THE STICKS AND BONES

SEANAN MCGUIRE

CENTER POINT LARGE PRINT
THORNDIKE, MAINE

The text of this Large Print edition is unabridged.
In other aspects, this book may vary
from the original edition.
Printed in the United States of America
on permanent paper.
Set in 16-point Times New Roman type.

ISBN: 978-1-64358-492-8

The Library of Congress has cataloged this record
under Library of Congress Control Number: 2019951753

FOR MEG

I think the rules were different there. It was all about science, but the science was magical. It didn't care about whether something could be done. It was about whether it should be done, and the answer was always, always yes.

—Jack Wolcott

PART I

JACK AND JILL
LIVE UP THE HILL

1 THE DANGEROUS ALLURE
OF OTHER PEOPLE'S CHILDREN

People who knew Chester and Serena Wolcott socially would have placed money on the idea that the couple would never choose to have children. They were not the parenting kind, by any reasonable estimation. Chester enjoyed silence and solitude when he was working in his home office, and viewed the slightest deviation from routine as an enormous, unforgiveable disruption. Children would be more than a slight deviation from routine. Children would be the nuclear option where routine was concerned. Serena enjoyed gardening and sitting on the board of various tidy, elegant nonprofits, and paying other people to maintain her home in a spotless state. Children were messes walking. They were trampled petunias and baseballs through picture windows, and they had no place in the carefully ordered world the Wolcotts inhabited.

What those people didn't see was the way the partners at Chester's law firm brought their sons to work, handsome little clones of their fathers in age-appropriate menswear, future kings of the world in their perfectly shined shoes, with their perfectly modulated voices. He watched, increasingly envious, as junior partners brought in pictures of their own sleeping sons and were lauded, and for what? Reproducing! Something so simple that any beast in the field could do it.

At night, he started dreaming of perfectly polite little boys with his hair and Serena's eyes, their blazers buttoned just *so,* the partners beaming beneficently at this proof of what a family man he was.

What those people didn't see was the way some of the women on Serena's boards would occasionally bring their daughters with them, making apologies about incompetent nannies or unwell babysitters, all while secretly gloating as everyone rushed to *ooh* and *ahh* over their beautiful baby girls. They were a garden in their own right, those privileged daughters in their gowns of lace and taffeta, and they would spend meetings and tea parties playing peacefully on the edge of the rug, cuddling their stuffed toys and feeding imaginary cookies to their dollies. Everyone she knew was quick to compliment those women for their sacrifices, and for what? Having a baby! Something so easy that people had been doing it since time began.

At night, she started dreaming of beautifully composed little girls with her mouth and Chester's nose, their dresses explosions of fripperies and frills, the ladies falling over themselves to be the first to tell her how wonderful her daughter was.

This, you see, is the true danger of children: they are ambushes, each and every one of them. A person may look at someone else's child and see only the surface, the shiny shoes or the perfect curls. They do not see the tears and the tantrums, the late nights, the sleepless hours, the worry. They do not even see the love, not really. It can be easy, when looking at children from the outside, to believe that they are things, dolls designed and programmed by their parents to behave in one manner, following one set of rules. It can be easy, when standing on the lofty shores of adulthood, not to remember that every adult was once a child, with ideas and ambitions of their own.

It can be easy, in the end, to forget that children are people, and that people will do what people will do, the consequences be damned.

It was right after Christmas—round after round of interminable office parties and charity events—when Chester turned to Serena and said, "I have something I would like to discuss with you."

"I want to have a baby," she replied.

Chester paused. He was an orderly man with an orderly wife, living in an ordinary, orderly life. He wasn't used to her being quite so open with her desires or, indeed, having desires at all.

It was dismaying . . . and a trifle exciting, if he were being honest.

Finally, he smiled, and said, "That was what I wanted to talk to you about."

There are people in this world—good, honest, hard-working people—who want nothing more than to have a baby, and who try for years to conceive one without the slightest success. There are people who must see doctors in small, sterile rooms, hearing terrifying proclamations about how much it will cost to even begin hoping. There are people who must go on quests, chasing down the north wind to ask for directions to the House of the Moon, where wishes can be granted, if the hour is right and the need is great enough. There are people who will try, and try, and try, and receive nothing for their efforts but a broken heart.

Chester and Serena went upstairs to their room, to the bed they shared, and Chester did not put on a condom, and Serena did not remind him, and that was that. The next morning, she stopped taking her birth control pills. Three weeks later, she missed her period, which had been as orderly and on-time as the rest of her life since she was twelve years old. Two weeks after that, she sat in a small white room while a kindly man in a long white coat told her that she was going to be a mother.

"How long before we can get a picture of the baby?" asked Chester, already imagining himself showing it to the men at the office, jaw strong, gaze distant, like he was lost in dreams of playing catch with his son-to-be.

"Yes, how long?" asked Serena. The women she worked with always shrieked and fawned when someone arrived with a new sonogram to pass around the group. How nice it would be, to finally be the center of attention!

The doctor, who had dealt with his share of eager parents, smiled. "You're about five weeks along," he said. "I don't recommend an ultrasound before twelve weeks, under normal circumstances. Now, this is your first pregnancy. You may want to wait before telling anyone that you're pregnant. Everything seems normal now, but it's early days yet, and it will be easier if you don't have to take back an announcement."

Serena looked bemused. Chester fumed. To even *suggest* that his wife might be so bad at being pregnant—something so simple that any fool off the street could do it—was offensive in ways he didn't even have words for. But Dr. Tozer had been recommended by one of the partners at his firm, with a knowing twinkle in his eye, and Chester simply couldn't see a way to change doctors without offending someone too important to offend.

"Twelve weeks, then," said Chester. "What do we do until then?"

Dr. Tozer told them. Vitamins and nutrition and reading, so much reading. It was like the man expected their baby to be the most difficult in the history of the world, with all the reading that he assigned. But they did it, dutifully, like they were following the steps of a magical spell that would summon the perfect child straight into their arms. They never discussed whether they were hoping for a boy or a girl; both of them knew, so completely, what they were going to have that it seemed unnecessary. So Chester went to bed each night dreaming of his son, while Serena dreamt of her daughter, and for a time, they both believed that parenthood was perfect.

They didn't listen to Dr. Tozer's advice about keeping the pregnancy a secret, of course. When something was this good, it needed to be shared. Their friends, who had never seen them as the parenting type, were confused but supportive. Their colleagues, who didn't know them well enough to understand what a bad idea this was, were enthusiastic. Chester and Serena shook their heads and made lofty comments about learning who their "real" friends were.

Serena went to her board meetings and smiled contently as the other women told her that she was beautiful, that she was glowing, that motherhood "suited her."

Chester went to his office and found that several of the partners were dropping by "just to chat" about his impending fatherhood, offering advice, offering camaraderie.

Everything was perfect.

They went to their first ultrasound appointment together, and Serena held Chester's hand as the technician rubbed blueish slime over her belly and rolled the wand across it. The picture began developing. For the first time, Serena felt a pang of concern. What if there was something wrong with the baby? What if Dr. Tozer had been right, and the pregnancy should have remained a secret, at least for a little while?

"Well?" asked Chester.

"You wanted to know the baby's gender, yes?" asked the technician.

He nodded.

"You have a perfect baby girl," said the technician.

Serena laughed in vindicated delight, the sound dying when she saw the scowl on Chester's face. Suddenly, the things they hadn't discussed seemed large enough to fill the room.

The technician gasped. "I have a second heartbeat," she said.

They both turned to look at her.

"Twins," she said.

"Is the second baby a boy or a girl?" asked Chester.

The technician hesitated. "The first baby is blocking our view," she hedged. "It's difficult to say for sure—"

"Guess," said Chester.

"I'm afraid it would not be ethical for me to guess at this stage," said the technician. "I'll make you another appointment, for two weeks from now. Babies move around in the womb. We should be able to get a better view then."

They did not get a better view. The first infant remained stubbornly in front, and the second infant remained stubbornly in back, and the Wolcotts made it all the way to the delivery room—for a scheduled induction, of course, the date chosen by mutual agreement and circled in their day planners—hoping quietly that they were about to become the proud parents of both son and daughter, completing their nuclear family on the first try. Both of them were slightly smug about the idea. It smacked of efficiency, of tailoring the perfect solution right out the gate.

(The thought that babies would become children, and children would become *people,* never occurred to them. The concept that perhaps biology was not destiny, and that not all little girls would be pretty princesses, and not all little boys would be brave soldiers, also never occurred to them. Things might have been easier if those ideas had ever slithered into their heads, unwanted but undeniably important. Alas, their minds were made up, and left no room for such revolutionary opinions.)

The labor took longer than planned. Serena did

not want a C-section if she could help it, did not want the scarring and the mess, and so she pushed when she was told to push, and rested when she was told to rest, and gave birth to her first child at five minutes to midnight on September fifteenth. The doctor passed the baby to a waiting nurse, announced, "It's a girl," and bent back over his patient.

Chester, who had been holding out hope that the reticent boy-child would push his way forward and claim the vaunted position of firstborn, said nothing as he held his wife's hand and listened to her straining to expel their second child. Her face was red, and the sounds she was making were nothing short of animal. It was horrifying. He couldn't imagine a circumstance under which he would touch her ever again. No; it was good that they were having both their children at once. This way, it would be over and done with.

A slap; a wail; and the doctor's voice proudly proclaiming, "It's another healthy baby girl!"

Serena fainted.

Chester envied her.

Later, when Serena was tucked safe in her private room with Chester beside her and the nurses asked if they wanted to meet their daughters, they said yes, of course. How could they have said anything different? They were parents now, and parenthood came with expectations.

Parenthood came with *rules*. If they failed to meet those expectations, they would be labeled unfit in the eyes of everyone they knew, and the consequences of *that,* well . . .

They were unthinkable.

The nurses returned with two pink-faced, hairless things that looked more like grubs or goblins than anything human. "One for each of you," twinkled a nurse, and handed Chester a tight-swaddled baby like it was the most ordinary thing in the world.

"Have you thought about names?" asked another, handing Serena the second infant.

"My mother's name was Jacqueline," said Serena cautiously, glancing at Chester. They had discussed names, naturally, one for a girl, one for a boy. They had never considered the need to name two girls.

"Our head partner's wife is named Jillian," said Chester. He could claim it was his mother's name if he needed to. No one would know. No one would ever know.

"Jack and Jill," said the first nurse, with a smile. "Cute."

"Jacqueline and Jillian," corrected Chester frostily. "No daughter of mine will go by something as base and undignified as a nickname."

The nurse's smile faded. "Of course not," she said, when what she really meant was "of course they will," and "you'll see soon enough."

Serena and Chester Wolcott had fallen prey to the dangerous allure of other people's children. They would learn the error of their ways soon enough. People like them always did.

2 PRACTICALLY PERFECT IN VIRTUALLY NO WAYS

The Wolcotts lived in a house at the top of a hill in the middle of a fashionable neighborhood where every house looked alike. The homeowner's association allowed for three colors of exterior paint (two colors too many, in the minds of many of the residents), a strict variety of fence and hedge styles around the front lawn, and small, relatively quiet dogs from a very short list of breeds. Most residents elected not to have dogs, rather than deal with the complicated process of filling out the permits and applications required to own one.

All of this conformity was designed not to strangle but to comfort, allowing the people who lived there to relax into a perfectly ordered world. At night, the air was quiet. Safe. Secure.

Save, of course, for the Wolcott home, where the silence was split by healthy wails from two sets of developing lungs. Serena sat in the dining room, staring blankly at the two screaming babies.

"You've had a bottle," she informed them.

"You've been changed. You've been walked around the house while I bounced you and sang that dreadful song about the spider. Why are you still *crying?*"

Jacqueline and Jillian, who were crying for some of the many reasons that babies cry—they were cold, they were distressed, they were offended by the existence of gravity—continued to wail. Serena stared at them in dismay. No one had told her that babies would *cry* all the time. Oh, there had been comments about it in the books she'd read, but she had assumed that they were simply referring to bad parents who failed to take a properly firm hand with their offspring.

"Can't you shut them up?" demanded Chester from behind her. She didn't have to turn to know that he was standing in the doorway in his dressing gown, scowling at all three of them—as if it were somehow *her* fault that babies seemed designed to scream without cease! He had been complicit in the creation of their daughters, but now that they were here, he wanted virtually nothing to do with them.

"I've been trying," she said. "I don't know what they want, and they can't tell me. I don't . . . I don't know what to do."

Chester had not slept properly in three days. He was starting to fear the moment when it would impact his work and catch the attention of the partners, painting him and his parenting abilities in a poor light. Perhaps it was desperation, or perhaps it was a moment of rare and impossible clarity.

"I'm calling my mother," he said.

Chester Wolcott was the youngest of three children: by the time he had come along, the mistakes had been made, the lessons had been learned, and his parents had been comfortable with the process of parenting. His mother was an unforgivably soppy, impractical woman, but she knew how to burp a baby, and perhaps by inviting her now, while Jacqueline and Jillian were too young to be influenced by her ideas about the world, they could avoid inviting her later, when she might actually do some damage.

Serena would normally have objected to the idea of her mother-in-law invading her home, setting everything out of order. With the babies screaming and the house already in disarray, all she could do was nod.

Chester made the call first thing in the morning.

Louise Wolcott arrived on the train eight hours later.

By the standards of anyone save for her ruthlessly regimented son, Louise was a disciplined, orderly woman. She liked the world to make sense and follow the rules. By the standards of her son, she was a hopeless dreamer. She thought the world was capable of kindness; she thought people were essentially good and

24

only waiting for an opportunity to show it.

She took a taxi from the train station to the house, because of course picking her up would have been a disruption to an already-disrupted schedule. She rang the bell, because of course giving her a key would have made no sense at all. Her eyes lit up when Serena answered the door, a baby in each arm, and she didn't even notice that her daughter-in-law's hair was uncombed, or that there were stains on the collar of her blouse. The things Serena thought were most important in the world held no relevance to Louise. Her attention was focused entirely on the babies.

"*There* they are," she said, as if the twins had been the subject of a global manhunt spanning years. She slipped in through the open door without waiting for an invitation, putting her suitcases down next to the umbrella stand (where they did *not* compliment the décor) before holding out her arms. "Come to Grandma," she said.

Serena would normally have argued. Serena would normally have insisted on offering coffee, tea, a place to put her bags where no one would have to see them. Serena, like her husband, had not slept a full night since coming home from the hospital.

"Welcome to our home," she said, and dumped both babies unceremoniously into Louise's arms before turning and walking up the stairs. The slam of the bedroom door followed a second later.

Louise blinked. She looked down at the babies. They had left off crying for the moment and were looking at her with wide, curious eyes. Their world was as yet fairly limited, and everything about it was new. Their grandmother was the newest thing of all. Louise smiled.

"Hello, darlings," she said. "I'm here now."

She would not leave for another five years.

The Wolcott house had been too big for Serena and Chester alone: they had rattled around in it like two teeth in a jar, only brushing against each other every so often. With two growing children and Chester's mother in the mix, the same house seemed suddenly too small.

Chester told the people at his work that Louise was a nanny, hired from a reputable firm to assist Serena, who had been overwhelmed by the difficulty of meeting the needs of twins. He spun her not as an inexperienced first-time mother but as a doting parent who had simply needed an extra pair of hands to meet the needs of her children. (The idea that he might have been that extra pair of hands never seemed to arise.)

Serena told the people on her boards that Louise was her husband's invalid mother, looking for a way to be useful while she recovered from her various non-contagious ailments. The twins were perfect angels, of course, she couldn't wish for better or more tractable children, but Louise needed *something* to do, and so it only made sense to let her play babysitter for a short while. (The idea of telling the truth was simply untenable. It would be tantamount to admitting failure, and Wolcotts did not *fail*.)

Louise told stories to Jacqueline and Jillian, told them they were clever, they were strong, they were miracles. She told them to sleep well and dry their eyes, and as they grew older, she told them to eat their vegetables and pick up their rooms, and always, always, she told them that she loved them. She told them that they were perfect exactly as they were, and that they would never need to change for anyone. She told them that they were going to change the world.

Gradually, Chester and Serena learned to tell their own daughters apart. Jacqueline had been the first born, and that seemed to have taken up all of her bravery; she was the more delicate of the two, hanging back and allowing her sister to go ahead of her. She was the first to learn to be afraid of the dark and start demanding a nightlight. She was the last to be weaned off the bottle, and she continued sucking her thumb long after Jillian had stopped.

Jillian, on the other hand, seemed to have been born with a deficit of common sense. There was no risk she wouldn't throw herself bodily against, from the stairs to the stove to the basement door. She had started walking with the abruptness of some children, going through none of the warning stages, and Louise had spent an afternoon chasing her around the house, padding the corners of the furniture, while Jacqueline had been lying comfortably in a sunbeam, oblivious to the danger her sister was courting.

(Serena and Chester had been furious when they came home from their daily distractions to find that all of their elegant, carefully chosen furniture now bore soft, spongy corners. It had taken Louise asking how many eyes they would like their daughters to have between them to convince them they should allow the childproofing to remain in place, at least for the time being.)

Unfortunately, with recognition came relegation. Identical twins were unsettling to much of the population: dressing them in matching outfits and treating them as one interchangeable being might seem appealing while they were young enough, but as they aged, they would start to unnerve people. Girls, especially, were subject to being viewed as alien or wrong when they seemed too alike. Blame science fiction, blame John Wyndham and Stephen King and Ira Levin. The fact remained that they needed to distinguish their daughters.

Jillian was quicker, wilder, more rough-and-tumble. Serena took her to the salon and brought her home with a pixie cut. Chester took her to the department store and brought her home with designer jeans, running shoes, and a puffy jacket that seemed almost bulkier than she was. Jillian, who was on the verge of turning four and idolized her often-distant parents as only a child could, modeled her new clothes for her wide-eyed, envious sister, and didn't think about what it meant for them to finally look different to people who weren't each other, or Gemma Lou, who had been able to tell them apart from the first day that she held them in her arms.

Jacqueline was slower, tamer, more cautious. Chester gave Serena his credit card, and she took their daughter to a store straight out of a fairy tale, where every dress was layered like a wedding cake and covered in cascades of lace and bows and glittering buttons, where every shoe was patent leather, and how they *shone*. Jacqueline, who was smart enough to know when something was wrong, came home dressed like a storybook, and clung to her sister, and cried.

"What a little tomboy she is!" people gushed when they saw Jillian—and because Jillian was young enough for being a tomboy to be cute, and endearing, and desirable, rather than something to judge, Chester beamed with pride. He might not have a son, but there were soccer leagues for girls. There were ways for her to impress the partners. A tough daughter was better than a weak son any day.

"What a little princess she is!" people gushed when they saw Jacqueline—and because that was all she had ever wanted from a daughter, Serena demurred and hid her smile behind her hand, soaking in the praise. Jacqueline was perfect. She would grow up just like the little girls that had inspired Serena to want one of her own, only better, because they would make none of the errors that other, lesser parents made.

(The idea that perhaps she and Chester hadn't made any errors in parenting because they hadn't really been parenting at all never occurred to her. She was their mother. Louise was a nanny at best, and a bad influence at worst. Yes, things had been difficult before Louise arrived, but that was just because she was recovering from childbirth. She would have picked up the necessary tricks of the trade quickly, if not for Louise hogging all the glory. She would.)

The twins began attending a half-day preschool when they were four and a half. Old enough to behave themselves in public; old enough to begin making the right friends, establishing the right connections. Jillian, who was brave within the familiar confines of her home and terrified of everything outside it, cried when Louise got them ready for their first day. Jacqueline, who had an endlessly curious mind and hungered for more to learn than one house could contain, did not. She stood silent and stoic in her frilly pink dress with the matching shoes, watching as Gemma Lou soothed her sister.

The idea of being jealous didn't occur to her. Jillian was getting more attention now, but she knew that meant that later, Gemma Lou would find an excuse to do something with just Jacqueline, something that would be just between them. Gemma Lou always knew when one twin was being left out, and she always made an effort to make up for it, to prevent gaps from forming. "There will come a day when you're all either of you has" was what she always said when one of them fussed about the other getting something. "Hold to that."

So they went off to preschool, and they held to each other until Jillian's fears were soothed away by the teacher, who had a pretty skirt and a pretty smile and smelled like vanilla. Then Jillian let go and ran off to play with a bunch of boys who had found a red rubber ball, while Jacqueline drifted into the corner occupied by girls whose pretty dresses were too tight to let them do more than stand around and admire one another.

They were all young. They were all shy. They stood in the corner like a flock of bright birds, and looked at each other out of the corners of their eyes, and watched as the louder, freer children rolled and tumbled on the floor, and if they were jealous, none of them said so.

But that night when she got home, Jacqueline kicked her dress under the bed, where it wouldn't be found until long after she had outgrown it, while Jillian sat in the corner with her arms full of dolls and refused to speak to anyone, not even Gemma Lou. The world was changing. They didn't like it.

They didn't know how to make it stop.

On Jacqueline and Jillian's fifth birthday, they had a cake with three tiers, covered in pink and purple roses and edible glitter. They had a party in the backyard with a bouncy castle and a table covered in gifts, and all the kids from their preschool were invited, along with all the children whose parents worked at Chester's firm, or served on one of Serena's boards. Many of them were older than the twins and formed their own little knots in corners of the yard or even inside, where they wouldn't have to listen to the younger children screaming.

Jillian loved having all her friends in her very own yard, where she knew the topography of the lawn and the location of all the sprinkler heads. She raced around like a wild thing, laughing and shrieking, and they raced with her, because that was how her friends had learned to play. Most of them were boys, too young to have learned about cooties and "no girls allowed." Louise watched from the back porch, frowning a little. She knew how cruel children could be, and she knew how much of Jillian's role was being forced upon her by her parents. In a year or two, the flow of things was going to change, and Jillian was going to find herself marooned.

Jacqueline held back, sticking close to Gemma, wary of getting dirt on her pretty dress, which had been chosen specifically for this event, and which she was under strict instructions to keep as clean as possible. She wasn't sure why—Jillian got covered in mud all the time, and it always washed out, so why couldn't they wash her dresses?—but she was sure there was a reason. There was always a reason, and it was never one her parents could explain to her.

Chester manned the barbecue, demonstrating his skill as a chef and a provider. Several of the partners were nearby, nursing beers and chatting about work. His chest felt like it was going to burst with pride. Here he was, the father in his own home, and there they were, the people he worked for, seeing how impressive his family was. He and Serena should have had children much sooner!

"Your daughter's a real scrapper, eh, Wolcott?"

"She is indeed," said Chester, flipping a burger. (The fact that he called people who did this for a living "burger-flippers" and looked down his nose at them was entirely lost on him, as it was on everyone around him.) "She's going to be a

33

spitfire when she gets a little older. We're already looking into peewee soccer leagues. She'll be an athlete when she grows up, just you wait and see."

"My wife would kill me if I tried to put our daughter in a pair of pants and send her off to play with the boys," said another partner, a wry chuckle in his voice. "You're a lucky man. Having two at once was the way to go."

"Absolutely," said Chester, as if they had planned this all along.

"Who's the old lady with your other daughter?" asked the first partner, nodding toward Louise. "Is that your nanny? She seems a little, well. Don't you think she's going to get tired, chasing two growing girls around all the time?"

"She's doing very well with them so far," said Chester.

"Well, keep an eye on her. You know what they say about old ladies: blink, and you'll be taking care of her instead of her taking care of your kids."

Chester flipped another burger, and said nothing at all.

On the other side of the yard, near the elegant, sugar-dusted cake, Serena moved in the center of a swarm of cooing society wives, and she had never felt more at home, or more like she was finally taking her proper place in the world. This had been the answer: children. Jacqueline and Jillian were unlocking the last of the doors that had stood between Serena and true social success—mostly Jacqueline, she felt, who was everything a young lady should be, quiet and sweet and increasingly polite with every year that passed. Why, some days she even forgot that Jillian was a girl, the contrast between them was so strong!

Some of the women she worked with were uncomfortable with the way she enforced Jacqueline's boundaries—usually the women who called her daughter "Jack" and encouraged her to do things like hunt for eggs on wet grass, or pet strange dogs that would shed on her dresses, dirtying them. Serena sniffed at them and calmly, quietly began moving their names down the various guest lists she controlled, until some of them had dropped off entirely. Those who remained had caught on quickly, after that, and stopped saying anything that smacked of criticism. What good was an opinion if it meant losing your place in society? No. Better to keep your mouth closed and your options open, that was what Serena always said.

She looked around the yard, searching for Jacqueline. Jillian was easy to find: as always, she was at the center of the largest degree of distasteful chaos. Jacqueline was harder. Finally, Serena spotted her in Louise's shadow, sticking close to her grandmother, as if the woman were the only person she trusted to protect her. Serena frowned.

The party was a success, as such things are reckoned: cake was eaten, presents were opened, bounces were bounced, two knees were skinned (belonging to two separate children), one dress was ruined, and one overexcited child failed to reach the bathroom before vomiting strawberry ice cream and vanilla cake all over the hall. When night fell, Jacqueline and Jillian were safely tucked in their room and Louise was in the kitchen, preparing herself a cup of tea. She heard footsteps behind her. She stopped, and turned, and frowned.

"Out with it," she said. "You know how Jill fusses if I'm not in my room when she comes looking for midnight kisses."

"Her name is Jillian, Mother, not Jill," said Chester.

"So you say," said Louise.

He sighed. "Please don't make this more difficult than it has to be."

"What, exactly?"

"We want to thank you for all the time you've spent helping with our children," said Chester. "They were a handful in the beginning. But I think we have things under control now."

Five is not where handfuls end, my boy, thought Louise. Aloud, she said, "Is that so?"

"Yes," said Serena. "Thank you so much, for

everything you've done. Don't you think you deserve the chance to rest?"

"There's nothing tiring about caring for children you love like your own," said Louise, but she had already lost, and she knew it. She had done her best. She had tried to encourage both girls to be themselves, and not to adhere to the rigid roles their parents were sketching a little more elaborately with every year. She had tried to make sure they knew that there were a hundred, a thousand, a million different ways to be a girl, and that all of them were valid, and that neither of them was doing anything wrong. She had tried.

Whether she had succeeded or not was virtually beside the point, because here were her son and his wife, and now she was going to leave those precious children in the hands of people who had never taken the time to learn anything about them beyond the most narrow, superficial things. They didn't know that Jillian was brave because she knew Jacqueline was always somewhere behind her with a careful plan for any situation that might arise. They didn't know that Jacqueline was timid because she was amused by watching the world deal with her sister, and thought the view was better from outside the splash radius.

(They also didn't know that Jacqueline was developing a slow terror of getting her hands dirty, thanks to them and their constant admonishments about protecting her dresses, which were too fancy by far for a child her age. They wouldn't have cared if she'd told them.)

"Mother, please," said Chester, and that was it: she'd lost.

Louise sighed. "When would you like me to go?" she asked.

"It would be best if you were gone when they woke up," said Serena, and that was that.

Louise Wolcott slipped out of her grand-daughters' lives as easily as she had slipped into them, becoming a distant name that sent birthday cards and the occasional gift (most confiscated by her son and daughter-in-law), and was one more piece of final, irrefutable proof that adults, in the end, were not and never to be trusted. There were worse lessons for the girls to learn.

This one, at least, might have a chance to save their lives.

3 THEY GROW UP SO FAST

Age six was kindergarten, where Jacqueline learned that little girls who wore frilly dresses every day were goody-goodies, not to be trusted, and Jillian learned that little girls who wore pants and ran around with the boys were weirdos and worse.

Age seven was first grade, where Jillian learned that she had cooties and smelled and no one wanted to play with her anyway, and Jacqueline learned that if she wanted people to like her, all she had to do was smile at them and say she liked their shoes.

Age eight was second grade, where Jacqueline learned that no one expected her to be smart if she was going to be pretty, and Jillian learned that everything about her was wrong, from the clothes she wore to the shows she watched.

"It must be *awful* to have such a dorky sister," said the girls in their class to Jacqueline, who felt like she should defend her sister, but didn't know how. Her parents had never given her the tools for loyalty, for sticking up or standing up or even sitting down (sitting down might muss her dress). So she hated Jillian a little, for being weird, for making things harder than they had to be, and she ignored the fact that it had been their parents all along, making their choices for them.

"It must be amazing to have such a pretty sister," said the boys in their class to Jillian (the ones who were still speaking to her, at least; the ones who had managed to get their cootie shots, and were starting to realize that girls were decorative, if nothing else). Jillian twisted in on herself, trying to figure out how she and her sister could share a face and a bedroom and a life, and still one of them was "the pretty one," and the other one was just Jillian, unwanted and ignored and increasingly being pushed from the role of "tomboy" and into the role of "nerd."

At night, they lay in their narrow, side-by-side beds and hated each other with the hot passion that could only exist between siblings, each of them wanting what the other had. Jacqueline wanted to run, to play, to be free. Jillian wanted to be liked, to be pretty, to be allowed to watch and listen, instead of always being forced to move. Each of them wanted people to *see* them, not an idea of them that someone else had come up with.

(A floor below them, Chester and Serena slept peacefully, untroubled by their choices. They had two daughters: they had two girls to mold into whatever they desired. The thought that they might be harming them by forcing them into narrow ideas of what a girl—of what a *person*—should be had never crossed their minds.)

By the time the girls turned twelve, it was easy for the people who met them to form swift, incorrect ideas of who they were as people. Jacqueline—*never* Jack; Jack was a knife of a name, short and sharp and cutting, without sufficient frills and flourishes for a girl like her—was quick-tongued and short-tempered, surrounded by sycophants who flocked to her from all sides of the school, eager to bask in the transitory warmth of her good graces. Most of the teachers thought that she was smarter than she let on, but virtually none of them could get her to show it. She was too afraid of getting dirty, of pencil smudges on her fingers and chalk dust on her cashmere sweaters. It was almost like she was afraid her mind was like a dress that couldn't be washed, and she didn't want to dirty it with facts she might not approve of later.

(The women on Serena's boards told her how lucky she was, how fortunate, and went home with their own daughters, and traded their party dresses for jeans, and never considered that Jacqueline Wolcott might not have the option.)

Jillian was quick-witted and slow-tempered, eager to please, constantly aching from rejection after rejection after rejection. The other girls wanted nothing to do with her, said that she was dirty from spending so much time playing with the boys, said that she wanted to be a boy herself, and that was why she didn't wear dresses, that was why she hacked off all her hair. The boys, standing on the precipice of puberty and besieged on all sides by their own sets of conflicting expectations, wanted nothing to do with her either. She wasn't pretty enough to be worth kissing (although a few of them had questioned how that could be, when she looked exactly like the prettiest girl in school), but she was still a girl, and their parents said that they shouldn't play with girls. So they'd cut her off, one by one, leaving her alone and puzzled and frightened of the world to come.

(The partners at Chester's firm told him how lucky he was, how fortunate, and went home to their own daughters, and watched them race around the backyard playing games of their own choosing, and never considered that Jillian Wolcott might not have any say in her own activities.)

The girls still shared a room; the girls were still friends, for all that the space between them was a minefield of resentment and resignation, always primed to explode. Every year, it got harder to remember that once they had been a closed unit, that neither of them had chosen the pattern of their life. Everything had been assigned. That didn't matter. Like bonsai being trained into shape by an assiduous gardener, they were growing into the geometry of their parents' desires, and it was pushing them further and further away from one another. One day, perhaps, one of them would reach across the gulf and find that there was no one there.

Neither of them was sure what they would do when that happened.

On the day our story truly starts—for surely none of that seemed like the beginning! Surely all of that was background, was explanation and justification for what's to come, as unavoidably as thunder follows lightning—it was raining. No: not raining. It was pouring, bucketing water from the sky like an incipient flood. Jacqueline and Jillian sat in their room, on their respective beds, and the room was so full of anger and of silence that it screamed.

Jacqueline was reading a book about fashionable girls having fashionable adventures at a fashionable school, and she thought that she couldn't possibly have been more bored. She occasionally cast narrow-eyed glances at the window, glaring at the rain. If the sky had been clear, she could have walked down the street to her friend Brooke's house. They could have painted each other's nails and talked about boys, a topic that Jacqueline found alternately fascinating and dull as dishwater, but which

Brooke always approached with the same unflagging enthusiasm. It would have been *something*.

Jillian, who had been intending to spend the day at soccer practice, sat on the floor next to her bed and moped so vigorously that it was like a gray cloud spreading across her side of the room. She couldn't go downstairs to watch television—no TV before four o'clock, not even on weekends, not even on rainy days—and she didn't have any books to read that she hadn't read five times already. She'd tried taking a look at one of Jacqueline's fashionable girl books, and had quickly found herself baffled at the number of ways the author found to describe everyone's hair. Maybe some things were worse than boredom after all.

When Jillian sighed for the fifth time in fifteen minutes, Jacqueline lowered her book and glowered at her across the room. "What *is* it?" she demanded.

"I'm bored," said Jillian mournfully.

"Read a book."

"I don't have any books I haven't read already."

"Read one of my books."

"I don't like your books."

"Go watch television."

"I'm not allowed for another hour."

"Play with your Lego."

"I don't feel like it." Jillian sighed heavily,

letting her head loll backward until it was resting against the edge of the bed. "I'm *bored*. I'm very *very* bored."

"You shouldn't say 'very' so much," said Jacqueline, parroting their mother. "It's a nonsense word. You don't need it."

"But it's true. I'm *very* very *very* bored."

Jacqueline hesitated. Sometimes the right thing to do with Jillian was wait her out: she would get distracted by something and peace would resume. Other times, the only way to handle her was to provide her with something to do. If something wasn't provided, she would *find* something, and it would usually be loud, and messy, and destructive.

"What do you want to do?" she asked finally.

Jillian gave her a sidelong, hopeful look. The days when her sister would willingly spend hours playing with her were long gone, as lost as the baseball cap she'd worn when she went to ride the carnival Scrambler with her father the summer before. The wind had taken the cap, and time had taken her sister's willingness to play hide-and-seek, or make-believe, or anything else their mother said was untidy.

"We could go play in the attic," she said finally, shyly, trying to keep herself from sounding like she hoped her sister would say yes. Hope only got you hurt. Hope was her least favorite thing, of all the things.

"There might be spiders," said Jacqueline. She wrinkled her nose, less out of actual distaste and more out of the knowledge that she was *supposed* to find spiders distasteful. She really found them rather endearing. They were sleek and clean and elegant, and when their webs got messed up, they ripped them down and started over again. People could learn a lot from spiders.

"I'll protect you, if there are," said Jill.

"We could get in trouble."

"I'll give you my desserts for three days," said Jill. Seeing that Jacqueline wasn't sold, she added, "And I'll do your dishes for a week."

Jacqueline *hated* doing the dishes. Of all the chores they were sometimes assigned, that was the worst. The dishes were bad enough, but the dishwater . . . it was like making her own personal swamp and then *playing* in it. "Deal," she said, and put her book primly aside, and slid off the bed.

Jillian managed not to clap in delight as she rose, grabbed her sister's hand, and hauled her out of the room. It was time for an adventure.

She had no idea how big an adventure it was going to be.

The Wolcott home was still far too large for the number of people it contained: large enough that Jacqueline and Jillian could each have had their own room, if they had wanted to, and never seen each other except for at the dinner table. They had started to worry, over the past year, that that would be their next birthday present: separate rooms, one pink and one blue, perfectly tailored to the children their parents wanted and not to the children that they had. They had been growing apart for years, following the paths that had been charted for them. Sometimes they hated each other and sometimes they loved each other, and both of them knew, deep down to the bone, that separate rooms would be the killing blow. They would always be twins. They would always be siblings. They might never be friends again.

Up the stairs they went, hand in hand, Jillian dragging Jacqueline, as had always been their way, Jacqueline making note of everything around them, ready to pull her sister back if danger loomed. The idea of being safe in their home had never occurred to either one of them. If they were seen—if their parents emerged from their room and saw the two of them moving through the house together—they would be separated, Jillian sent off to play in the puddles out back, Jacqueline returned to their room to read her books and sit quietly, not disturbing anything.

They were starting to feel, in a vague, unformed way, as if their parents were doing something wrong. Both of them knew kids who were the way they were supposed to be, girls who loved pretty dresses and sitting still, or who loved mud and shouting and kicking a ball. But they also knew girls who wore dresses while they terrorized the tetherball courts, and girls who wore sneakers and jeans and came to school with backpacks full of dolls in gowns of glittering gauze. They knew boys who liked to stay clean, or who liked to sit and color, or who joined the girls with the backpacks full of dolls in their corners. Other children were allowed to be mixed up, dirty *and* clean, noisy *and* polite, while they each had to be just one thing, no matter how hard it was, no matter how much they wanted to be something else.

It was an uncomfortable thing, feeling like their parents weren't doing what was best for them; like this house, this vast, perfectly organized house, with its clean, artfully decorated rooms, was pressing the life out of them one inch at a time. If they didn't find a way out, they were going to become paper dolls, flat and faceless and ready to be dressed however their parents wanted them to be.

At the top of the stairs there was a door that they weren't supposed to go through, leading to a room that they weren't supposed to remember. Gemma Lou had lived there when they were little, before they got to be too much trouble and she forgot how to love them. (That was what their mother said, anyway, and Jillian believed it, because Jillian knew that love was always conditional; that there was always, always a catch. Jacqueline, who was quieter and hence saw more that she wasn't supposed to see, wasn't so sure.) The door was always locked, but the key had been thrown into the kitchen junk drawer after Gemma Lou left, and Jacqueline had quietly stolen it on their seventh birthday, when she had finally felt strong enough to remember the grandmother who hadn't loved them enough to stay.

Since then, when they needed a place to hide from their parents, a place where Chester and Serena wouldn't think to look, they had retreated to Gemma Lou's room. There was still a bed there, and the drawers of the dresser smelled like her perfume when they were opened, and she had left an old steamer trunk in the closet, filled with clothes and costume jewelry that she had been putting aside for her granddaughters, waiting for the day when they'd be old enough to play make-believe and fashion show with her as their appreciative audience. It was that trunk that had convinced them both that Gemma Lou hadn't always intended to leave. Maybe she'd forgotten how to love them and maybe she hadn't, but once upon a time, she had been planning to stay. That anyone would ever have planned to stay for their sake meant the world.

Jacqueline unlocked the door and tucked the

key into her pocket, where it would be secure, because she never lost anything. Jillian opened the door and took the first step into the room, making sure their parents weren't lurking for them there, because she was always the first one past the threshold. Then the door was closed behind them, and they were finally safe, truly safe, with no roles to play except for the ones they chose for themselves.

"I call dibs on the pirate sword," said Jacqueline excitedly, and ran for the closet, grabbing the lid of the trunk and shoving it upward. Then she stopped, elation fading into confusion. "Where did the clothes go?"

"What?" Jillian crowded in next to her sister, peering into the trunk. The dress-up clothes and accessories were gone, all of them, replaced by a winding wooden staircase that descended down, down, down into the darkness.

Had Gemma Lou been allowed to stay with them, they might have read more fairy tales, might have heard more stories about children who opened doors to one place and found themselves stepping through into another. Had they been allowed to grow according to their own paths, to follow their own interests, they might have met Alice, and Peter, and Dorothy, all the children who had strayed from the path and found themselves lost in someone else's fairyland. But fairy tales had been too bloody and violent for

Serena's tastes, and children's books had been too soft and whimsical for Chester's tastes, and so somehow, unbelievable as it might seem, Jacqueline and Jillian had never been exposed to the question of what might be lurking behind a door that wasn't supposed to be there.

The two of them looked at the impossible stairway and were too baffled and excited to be afraid.

"Those weren't there last time," said Jillian.

"Maybe they were, and the dresses were just all on top of them," said Jacqueline.

"The dresses would have fallen," said Jillian.

"Don't be stupid," said Jacqueline—but it was a fair point, wasn't it? If there had always been stairs in the trunk, then all the things Gemma Lou had left for them would have fallen. Unless . . . "There's a lid here," she said. "Maybe there's a lid on the bottom, too, and it came open, and everything fell down the stairs."

"Oh," said Jillian. "What should we do?"

Dimly, Jacqueline was beginning to realize that this wasn't just a mystery: it was an *opportunity*. Their parents didn't know there was a stairway hidden in Gemma Lou's old closet. They couldn't know. If they *had* known, they would have put the key somewhere much harder to find than the kitchen junk drawer. The stairs looked dusty, like no one had walked on them in years and years, and Serena *hated* dust, which meant she didn't know that the stairs existed. If Jacqueline and Jillian went down those stairs, why, they would be walking into something secret. Something new. Something their parents had maybe never seen and couldn't fence in with inexplicable adult rules.

"We should go and find all our dress-up clothes and put them away, so that we're not making a mess in Gemma Lou's room," said Jacqueline, as if it were the most reasonable thing in the world.

Jillian frowned. There was something in her sister's logic that didn't sit right with her. She was fine with sneaking into their grandmother's room, because they had been welcome there before Gemma Lou had stopped loving them and gone away; this was their place as much as it had been hers. The stairs in the trunk, on the other hand . . . those were something new and strange and alien. Those belonged to someone other than Gemma Lou, and someone other than them.

"I don't know . . ." she said warily.

Perhaps, if the sisters had been encouraged to love each other more, to trust each other more, to view each other as something other than competition for the limited supplies of their parents' love, they would have closed the trunk and gone to find an adult. When they had led their puzzled parents back to Gemma Lou's room, opening the trunk again would have revealed no secrets, no stairs, just a mess of dress-up clothes, and the confusion that always follows when something magical disappears. Perhaps.

But that hadn't been their childhood: that hadn't been their life. They were competitors as much as they were companions, and the thought of telling their parents would never have occurred to them.

"Well, *I'm* going," said Jacqueline, with a prim sniff, and slung her leg over the edge of the trunk.

It was easier than she had expected it to be. It was like the trunk *wanted* her to step inside, like the stairs *wanted* her to descend them. She climbed through the opening and went down several steps before smoothing her dress with the heels of her hands, looking back over her shoulder, and asking, "Well?"

Jillian was not as brave as everyone had always assumed she was. She was not as wild as everyone had always wanted her to be. But she had spent her life so far being told that she was both those things, and more, that her sister was neither of them; if there was an adventure to be had, she simply could not allow Jacqueline to have it without her. She hoisted herself over the edge of the trunk, tumbling in her hurry, and came to a stop a step above where Jacqueline was waiting.

"I'm coming with you," she said, picking herself up without bothering to dust herself off.

Jacqueline, who had been expecting this outcome, nodded and offered her hand to her sister.

"So neither one of us gets lost," she said.

Jillian nodded, and took her sister's hand, and together they walked down, down, down into the dark.

The trunk waited until they were too far down to hear before it swung closed, shutting them in, shutting the old world out. Neither of the girls noticed. They just kept on descending.

Some adventures begin easily. It is not *hard,* after all, to be sucked up by a tornado or pushed through a particularly porous mirror; there is no skill involved in being swept away by a great wave or pulled down a rabbit hole. Some adventures require nothing more than a willing heart and the ability to trip over the cracks in the world.

Other adventures must be committed to before they have even properly begun. How else will they know the worthy from the unworthy, if they do not require a certain amount of effort on the part of the ones who would undertake them? Some adventures are cruel, because it is the only way they know to be kind.

Jacqueline and Jillian descended the stairs until their legs ached and their knees knocked and their mouths were dry as deserts. An adult in their place might have turned around and gone back the way they had come, choosing to retreat to the land of familiar things, of faucets that ran wet with water, of safe, flat surfaces. But they were children, and the logic of children said that it was easier to go down than it was to go up. The logic of children ignored the fact that one day, they would have to climb back up, into the light, if they wanted to go home.

When they were halfway down (although they didn't know it; each step was like the last), Jillian slipped and fell, her hand wrenched out of Jacqueline's. She cried out, sharp and wordless, as she tumbled down, and Jacqueline chased after her, until they huddled together, bruised and slightly stunned, on one of the infrequent landings.

"I want to go back," sniffled Jillian.

"Why?" asked Jacqueline. There was no good answer, and so they resumed their descent, down, down, down, down past earthen walls thick with tree roots and, later, with the great white bones of beasts that had walked the Earth so long ago that it might as well have been a fairy tale.

Down, down, down they went, two little girls who couldn't have been more different, or more the same. They wore the same face; they viewed the world through the same eyes, blue as the sky after a storm. They had the same hair, white-blonde, pale enough to seem to glow in the dim light of the stairway, although Jacqueline's hung in long corkscrew curls, while Jillian's was cut short, exposing her ears and the elegant line of her neck. They both stood, and moved, cautiously, as if expecting correction to come at any moment.

Down, down, down they went, until they stepped off the final stair, into a small, round room with bones and roots embedded in the walls, with dim white lights on strings hanging around the edges of it, like Christmas had been declared early. Jacqueline looked at them and thought of mining lights, of dark places underground. Jillian looked at them and thought of haunted houses, of places that took more than they gave. Both girls shivered, stepping closer together.

There was a door. It was small, and plain, and made of rough, untreated pine. A sign hung at adult eye level. BE SURE, it said, in letters that looked like they had been branded into the wood.

"Be sure of what?" asked Jillian.

"Be sure that we want to see what's on the other side, I guess," said Jacqueline. "There isn't any other way to go."

"We could go back up."

Jacqueline looked flatly at her sister. "My legs hurt," she said. "Besides, I thought you wanted an adventure. 'We found a door, but we didn't like it, so we went back without seeing what was on the other side' isn't an adventure. It's . . . it's running away."

"I don't run away," said Jillian.

"Good," said Jacqueline, and reached for the doorknob.

It turned before she could grab it, and the door swung open, revealing the most impossible place either girl had ever seen in their life.

It was a field. A big field, so big that it seemed like it went on just shy of forever—and the only reason it didn't go on farther was because it ran up against the edge of what looked like an ocean, slate-gray and dashing itself against a rocky, unforgiving shore. Neither girl knew the word for "moor," but if they had, they would have both agreed in an instant that this was a moor. This was *the* moor, the single platonic ideal from which all other moors had been derived. The ground was rich with a mixture of low-growing shrubs and bright-petaled flowers, growing blue and orange and purple, a riot of impossible color. Jillian stepped forward with a small sound of amazement and delight. Jacqueline, not wanting to be left behind, followed her.

The door slammed shut behind them. Neither girl noticed, not yet. They were busy running through the flowers, laughing, under the eye of the vast and bloody moon.

Their story had finally begun.

PART II

JILL AND JACK
INTO THE BLACK

4 TO MARKET, TO MARKET, TO BUY A FAT HEN

Jillian and Jacqueline ran through the flowers like wild things—and in that moment, that brief and shining moment, with their parents far away and unaware of what their daughters were doing, with no one who dwelt in the Moors yet aware of their existence, they *were* wild things, free to do whatever they wanted, and what they wanted to do was *run*.

Jacqueline ran like she had been saving all her running for this moment, for this place where no one could see her, or scold her, or tell her that ladies didn't behave that way, sit down, slow down, you'll rip your dress, you'll stain your tights, be *good*. She was getting grass stains on her knees and mud under her fingernails, and she knew she'd regret both those things later, but in the moment, she didn't care. She was finally running. She was finally free.

Jillian ran more slowly, careful not to trample the flowers, slowing down whenever she felt like it to look around herself in wide-eyed wonder. No one was telling her to go faster, to run harder, to keep her eyes on the ball; no one wanted this to be a competition. For the first time in years, she was running solely for the joy of running, and when she tripped and fell into the flowers, she went down laughing.

Then she rolled onto her back and the laughter stopped, drying up in her throat as she stared, wide-eyed, at the vast ruby eye of the moon.

Now, those of you who have seen the moon may think you know what Jillian saw: may think that you can picture it, shining in the sky above her. The moon is the friendliest of the celestial bodies, after all, glowing warm and white and welcoming, like a friend who wants only to know that all of us are safe in our narrow worlds, our narrow yards, our narrow, well-considered lives. The moon worries. We may not know how we know that, but we know it all the same: that the moon watches, and the moon worries, and the moon will always love us, no matter what.

This moon watched, but that was where the resemblance to the clean and comfortable moon that had watched over the twins all the days of their lives ended. This moon was huge, and red as a ruby somehow set into the night sky, surrounded by the gleaming points of a million stars. Jillian had never in her life seen so many stars. She stared at them as much as at the moon, which seemed to be *looking* at her with a focus and intensity that she had never noticed before.

Gradually, Jacqueline tired of running, and moved to sit down next to her sister in the flowers. Jillian pointed mutely upward. Jacqueline looked, and frowned, suddenly uneasy.

"The moon is wrong," she said.

"It's red," said Jillian.

"No," said Jacqueline—who had, after all, been encouraged to sit quietly, to read books rather than play noisy games, to *watch*. No one had ever thought to ask her to be smart, which was good, in the grand scheme of things: her mother would have been much more likely to ask her to be a little foolish, because foolish girls were more tractable than stubbornly clever ones. Cleverness was a boy's attribute, and would only get in the way of sitting quietly and being mindful.

Jacqueline had found cleverness all on her own, teasing it out of the silences she found herself marooned in, using it to fill the gaps naturally created by a life lived being good, and still, and patient. She was only twelve years old. There were limits to the things she knew. And yet . . .

"The moon shouldn't be that big," she said. "It's too far away to be that big. It would have to be so close that it would mess up all the tides and pull the world apart, because gravity."

"Gravity can do that?" asked Jillian, horrified.

"It could, if the moon were that close," said Jacqueline. She stood, leaning down to pull her sister along with her. "We shouldn't be here."

The moon was wrong, and there were mountains in the distance. *Mountains*. Somehow, she didn't have a problem with the idea that there was a field and an ocean below the basement, but mountains? That was a step too far.

"The door's gone," said Jillian. She had a sprig of some woody purple plant in her hair, like a barrette. It was pretty. Jacqueline couldn't think of the last time she'd seen her sister wearing something just because it was pretty. "How are we supposed to go home if the door's gone?"

"If the moon can be wrong, the door can move," said Jacqueline, with what she hoped would sound like certainty. "We just need to find it."

"Where?"

Jacqueline hesitated. The ocean was in front of them, big and furious and stormy. The waves would carry them away in an instant, if they got too close. The mountains were behind them, tall and craggy and foreboding. Shapes that looked like castles perched on the highest peaks. Even if they could climb that far, there was no guarantee that the people who lived in castles like grasping hands, high up the slope of a mountain, would ever be friendly toward two lost little girls.

"We can go left or we can go right," said Jacqueline finally. "You choose."

Jillian lit up. She couldn't remember the last time her sister had asked her to choose something, had trusted her not to lead them straight into a mud puddle or other small disaster. "Left," she said, and grabbed her sister's hand, and hauled her away across the vast and menacing moor.

It is important to understand the world in which Jacqueline and Jillian found themselves marooned, even if they would not understand it fully for some time, if ever. And so, the Moors:

There are worlds built on rainbows and worlds built on rain. There are worlds of pure mathematics, where every number chimes like crystal as it rolls into reality. There are worlds of light and worlds of darkness, worlds of rhyme and worlds of reason, and worlds where the only thing that matters is the goodness in a hero's heart. The Moors are none of those things. The Moors exist in eternal twilight, in the pause between the lightning strike and the resurrection. They are a place of endless scientific experimentation, of monstrous beauty, and of terrible consequences.

Had the girls turned toward the mountains, they would have found themselves in a world washed in snow and pine, where the howls of wolves split the night, and where the lords of eternal winter ruled with an unforgiving hand.

Had the girls turned toward the sea, they would have found themselves in a world caught forever at the moment of drowning, where the songs of sirens lured the unwary to their deaths, and where the lords of half-sunken manors never forgot, or forgave, those who trespassed against them.

But they did neither of those things. Instead, they walked through brush and bracken, pausing occasionally to gather flowers that they had never seen before, flowers that bloomed white as bone, or yellow as bile, or with the soft suggestion of a woman's face tucked into the center of their petals. They walked until they could walk no more, and when they curled together in their exhaustion, the undergrowth made a lovely mattress, while the overgrowth shielded them from casual view.

The moon set. The sun rose, bringing storm clouds with it. It hid behind them all through the day, so that the sky was never any brighter than it had been when they arrived. Wolves came down from the mountains and unspeakable things came up from the sea, all gathering around the sleeping children and watching them dream the hours away. None made a move to touch the girls. They had made their choice: they had chosen the Moors. Their fate, and their future, was set.

When the moon rose again the beasts of mountain and sea slipped away, leaving Jacqueline and Jillian to wake to a lonely, silent world.

Jillian was the first to open her eyes. She looked up at the red moon hanging above them, and was surprised twice in the span of a second: first by how close the moon still looked, and second by her lack of surprise at their location. Of course this was all real. She had had her share of wild and beautiful dreams, but never anything like this. And if she hadn't dreamed it, it had to be real, and if it was real, of course they were still there. Real places didn't go away just because you'd had a nap.

Beside her, Jacqueline stirred. Jillian turned to her sister, and grimaced at the sight of a slug making its slow way along the curve of Jacqueline's ear. They were having an adventure, and it would all be spoiled if Jacqueline started to panic over getting dirty. Careful as anything, Jillian reached over and plucked the slug from her sister's ear, flicking it into the brush.

When she looked back, Jacqueline's eyes were open. "We're still here," she said.

"Yes," said Jillian.

Jacqueline stood, scowling at the grass stains on her knees, the mud on the hem of her dress. It was a good thing she couldn't see her own hair, thought Jillian; she would probably have started crying if she could.

"We need to find a door," said Jacqueline.

"Yes," said Jillian, and she didn't mean it, and when Jacqueline offered her hand, she took it anyway, because they were together, the two of them, really *together,* and even if that couldn't last, it was still novel and miraculous. When people heard that she had a twin, they were always quick to say how nice that had to be, having a best friend from birth. She had never been able to figure out how to tell them how wrong they were. Having a twin meant always having someone to be compared to and fall short of, someone who was under no obligation to like you—and wouldn't, most of the time, because emotional attachments were dangerous.

(Had she been able to articulate how she felt about her home life, had she been able to tell an adult, Jillian might have been surprised by the way things could change. But ah, if she had done that, she and her sister would never have become the bundle of resentments and contradictions necessary to summon a door to the Moors. Every choice feeds every choice that comes after, whether we want those choices or no.)

Jacqueline and Jillian walked across the moorland hand in hand. They didn't talk, because they didn't know what there was to talk about: the easy conversation of sisters had stopped coming easily to them almost as soon as they had learned to speak. But they took comfort in being together, in the knowledge that neither one of them was making this journey alone. They took comfort in proximity. After their semi-shared childhood, that was the closest they could come to enjoying one another's company.

The ground was uneven, as rocky heaths and

moorlands often are. They had been climbing for a little while, coming to the end of the flat plain. At the crest of the hill Jacqueline's foot hit a dip in the soil, and she fell, tumbling down the other side of the hill with a speed as surprising as it was bruising. Jillian shouted her sister's name, lunging for her hand, and found herself falling as well, two little girls rolling end over end, like stars tumbling out of an overcrowded sky.

In places like the Moors, when the red moon is looking down from the sky and making choices about the story, when the travelers have made their decisions about which way to go, distance is sometimes more of an idea than an enforceable law. The girls tumbled to a stop, Jacqueline landing on her front and Jillian landing on her back, both with queasy stomachs and heads full of spangles. They sat up, reaching for each other, brushing the heath out of their eyes, and gaped in open-mouthed amazement at the wall that had suddenly appeared in front of them.

A word must be said, about the wall.

Those of us who make our homes in the modern world, where there are very few monsters roaming the fens, very few werewolves howling in the night, think we understand the nature of walls. They are dividing lines between one room and another, more of a courtesy than anything else. Some people have chosen to do away with them altogether, living life in what they call an "open floor plan." Privacy and protection are ideas, not necessities, and a wall outside is better called a fence.

This was no fence. This was a *wall,* in the oldest, truest sense of the word. Entire trees had been cut down, sharpened into stakes and driven into the ground. They were bound together with iron and with hand-woven ropes, the spaces between them sealed with concrete that glittered oddly in the moonlight, like it was made of something more than simply stone. An army could have run aground against that wall, unable to go any farther.

There was a gate in the wall, closed against the night, as vast and intimidating as the scrubland around it. Looking at that gate, it was difficult to believe that it would ever open, or that it *could* ever open. It seemed more like a decorative flourish than a functional thing.

"Whoa," said Jillian.

Jacqueline was cold. She was bruised. Worst of all, she was *dirty*. She had, quite simply, Had Enough. And so she marched forward, out of the bracken, onto the hard-packed dirt surrounding the wall, and she knocked as hard on the gate as her soft child's hands would allow. Jillian gasped, grabbing her arm and dragging her back.

But the damage, such as it was, had been done. The gate creaked open, splitting down the middle to reveal a medieval-looking courtyard. There was a fountain in the center, a bronze-and-steel statue of a man in a long cloak, his pensive gaze fixed upon the high mountains. No one stirred. It was a deserted place, an abandoned place, and looking at it filled Jillian's heart with dread.

"We shouldn't be here," she murmured.

"Indeed, you probably should not," said a man's voice. Both girls screamed and jumped, whirling around to find the man from the fountain standing behind them, looking at them like they were a strange new species of insect found crawling around his garden.

"But you *are* here," he continued. "That means, I suppose, that I'll have to deal with you."

Jacqueline reached for Jillian's hand, found it, and held fast, both of them staring in mute fear at the stranger.

He was a tall man, taller than their father, who had always been the tallest point in their world. He was a handsome man, like something out of a movie (although Jacqueline wasn't sure she'd ever seen a movie star so pale, or so seemingly sculpted out of some cold white substance). His hair was very black, and his eyes were orange, like jack-o'-lanterns. Most surprising of all was his red, red mouth, which looked like it had been painted, like he was wearing lipstick.

The lining of his cloak was the same red color as his mouth, and his suit was as black as his hair, and he held himself so perfectly still that he didn't seem human.

"Please, sir, we didn't mean to go anywhere we aren't supposed to be," said Jillian, who had, after all, spent years pretending she knew how to be brave. She tried so hard that sometimes she forgot that she was lying. "We thought we were still in our house."

The man tilted his head, like he was looking at a very interesting bug, and asked, "Does your house normally include an entire world? It must be quite large. You must spend a great deal of time dusting."

"There was a door," said Jacqueline, coming to her sister's defense.

"Was there? And was there, by any chance, a sign on the door? An instruction, perhaps?"

"It said . . . it said 'be sure,'" said Jacqueline.

"Mmm." The man inclined his head. It wasn't a nod; more a form of acknowledgment that someone else had spoken. "And were you?"

"Were we what?" asked Jillian.

"Sure," he said.

The girls stepped a little closer together, suddenly cold. They were tired and they were hungry and their feet hurt, and nothing this man said was making any sense.

"No," they said, in unison.

The man actually smiled. "Thank you," he said, and his voice was not unkind.

Maybe that was what gave Jillian the courage to ask, "For what?"

"For not lying to me," he said. "What are your names?"

"Jacqueline," said Jacqueline, and "Jillian," said Jillian, and the man, who had seen his share of children come walking through those hills, come knocking at those gates, smiled.

"Jack and Jill came down the hill," he said. "You must be hungry. Come with me."

The girls exchanged a look, uneasy, although they could not have said why. But they were only twelve, and the habits of obedience were strong in them.

"All right," they said, and when he walked through the gates into the empty square, they followed him, and the gates swung shut behind them, shutting out the scrubland. They could not shut out the disapproving red eye of the moon, which watched, and judged, and said nothing.

5 THE ROLES WE CHOOSE OURSELVES

The man led them through the silent town beyond the wall. Jill kept her eyes on him as she walked, trusting that if anything were to happen, it would begin with the only person they had seen since climbing into the bottom of their grandmother's trunk. Jack, who was more used to silence, and stillness, and found it less distracting, watched the windows. She saw the flicker of candles as they were moved hastily out of view; she saw the curtains sway, as if they had just been released by an unseen hand.

They were not alone there, and the people they shared the evening with were all in hiding. But why? Surely two little girls and a man who wore a cape couldn't be *that* frightening. And she was hungry, and cold, and tired, and so she kept her mouth closed and followed along until they came to a barred iron door in a gray stone wall. The man turned to look at them, his expression grave.

"This is your first night in the Moors, and the law says I must extend to you the hospitality of my home for the duration of three moonrises," he said solemnly. "During that time, you will be as safe under my roof as I am. No one will harm you. No one will hex you. No one will draw upon your blood. When that time is done, you will be subject to the laws of this land, and will pay for what you take as would anyone. Do you understand?"

"What?" said Jill.

"No," said Jack. "That doesn't . . . What do you mean, 'draw upon our blood'? Why would you be doing anything with our blood?"

"What?" said Jill.

"We're not even going to *be* here in three days. We just need to find a door, and then we're going to go home. Our parents are worried about us." It was the first lie Jack had told since coming to the Moors, and it stuck in her throat like a stone.

"What?" said Jill, for the third time.

The man smiled. His teeth were as white as his lips were red, and for the first time, the contrast seemed to put some color into his skin. "Oh, this will be fun," he said, and opened the iron door.

On the other side was a hall. It was a perfectly normal hall, as subterranean castle halls went: the walls were stone, the floor was carpeted in faded red and black filigree, and the chandeliers that hung from the ceiling were rich with spider webs, tangled perilously close to the burning candles. The man stepped through. Jack and Jill, lacking any better options, followed him.

See them now as they were then, two golden-haired little girls in torn and muddy clothes, following a spotless stranger through the castle. See how he moves, as fluid as a hunting cat, his feet barely seeming to brush the ground, and how the children hurry to keep up with him, almost tripping over themselves in their eagerness to not be left behind! They are still holding each other's hands, our lost little girls, but already Jack is beginning to lag a little, suspicious of their host, wary of what happens when the three days are done.

They are not twins who have been taught the importance of cleaving to each other, and the cracks between them are already beginning to show. It will not be long before they are separated.

But ah, that is the future, and this is the present. The man walked and Jack and Jill followed, already wearing their shortened names like the armor that they would eventually become. Jack had always been "Jacqueline," avoiding the short, sharp, masculine sound of "Jack" (and her mother had asked, more than once, whether there was a way to trade the names between the girls, to make Jacqueline Jillian, to let Jillian be Jack). Jill had always been "Jillian," clinging to the narrow blade of femininity that she had been allowed, refusing to be truncated (and her father had looked into the question of name changes, only to dismiss it as overly complicated, for insufficient gain). Jill dogged their guide's heels and Jack hung back as much as their joined hands allowed, and when they reached a flight of stairs, narrower than the one that had brought them there, made of stone instead of dusty wood, they both stopped for a moment, looking at the steps in silence.

The man paused to look at them, a smile toying with the corner of his mouth. "This is not the way home for you, little foundlings," he said. "I'm afraid that will be more difficult to find than the stairs that connect my village to my dining room."

"*Your* village?" asked Jack, forgetting to be afraid in her awe. "The whole thing? You own the whole thing?"

"Every stick and every bone," said the man. "Why? Does that impress you?"

"A bit," she admitted.

The man's smile grew. She was very lovely, after all, with hair like sunlight and the sort of smooth skin that spoke of days spent mostly indoors, away from the weather. She would be tractable; she would be sweet. She might do.

"I have many impressive things," he said, and started up the stairs, leaving the girls with little choice but to follow him unless they wanted to be left behind.

Up they went, up and up and up until it felt

like they must have climbed all the way back to the bottom of Gemma Lou's trunk, back into the familiar confines of their own house. Instead, they emerged from the stairwell and into a beautiful dining room. The long mahogany table was set for one. The maid standing near the far wall looked alarmed when the man stepped into the room, trailed by two little girls. She started to step forward, only to stop herself and stand there, wringing her hands.

"Peace, Mary, peace," said the man. "They're travelers—foundlings. They came through a door, and this is their first night of three."

The woman didn't look reassured. If anything, she looked more concerned. "They're quite dirty," she said. "Best give them to me, so's I can give them a bath, and they don't disturb your dinner."

"Don't be silly," he said. "They're eating with me. Notify the kitchen that I'll require two plates of whatever it is that children eat."

"Yes, m'lord," said Mary, bobbing a quick and anxious curtsey. She was not old, but she was not young either; she looked like one of the neighborhood women who were sometimes hired to watch Jack and Jill during the summer, when their parents had to work. Camp was too messy and loud for Jack, and summer enrichment programs could only fill so many hours of the day. Childcare, distasteful as it was, was sometimes the only option.

(Age was the only thing Mary had in common with those poised and perfect ladies, who always came with credentials and references and carpetbags filled with activities for them to share. Mary's hair was brown and curly and looked as likely to steal a hairbrush as it was to yield before it. Her eyes were the cloudy gray of used dishwater, and she stood at the sort of rigid attention that spoke of bone-deep exhaustion. Had she shown up on the doorstep seeking work, Serena Wolcott would have turned her away on sight. Jack trusted her instantly. Jill did not.)

Mary gave the girls one last anxious look before heading for the door on the other side of the room. She was almost there when the man cleared his throat, stopping her dead in her tracks.

"Tell Ivan to send for Dr. Bleak," he said. "I haven't forgotten our agreement."

"Yes, m'lord," she said, and she was gone.

The man turned to Jack and Jill, smiling when he saw how intently they were watching him. "Dinner will be ready soon, and I'm sure that you will find it to your liking," he said. "Don't let Mary frighten you. Three days I promised, and three days you'll have, before you need to fear anything within these walls."

"What happens when the three days are over?" asked Jill, who had long since learned that games had rules, and that rules needed to be followed.

"Come," said the man. "Sit."

He walked to the head of the table, where he settled at the place that had been set for him. Jill sat on his left. Jack moved to sit beside her, and he shook his head, indicating the place on his right.

"If I'm to have a matching pair for three days, I may as well enjoy it," he said. "Don't worry. There's nothing to fear from me." The word *yet* seemed to hang, unspoken but implied, over the three of them.

But ah, Jack had seen very few horror movies in her day, and Jill, who might have been better prepared to interpret the signs, was exhausted and overwhelmed and still dizzy with the novelty of spending a day in the company of her sister without fighting. They sat where they were told, and they were still sitting there when Mary returned, followed by two silent, hollow-cheeked men in black tailcoats that hung almost to their knees. Each of the men was carrying a silver-domed plate.

"Ah, good," said the man. "How were these prepared?"

"The kitchen-witch conjured things that are pleasing to children," said Mary, voice stiff, chin raised. "She promises their satisfaction."

"Excellent," said the man. "Girls? Which will you have?"

"The left, please," said Jill, remembering every scrap of manners she had ever possessed. Her stomach rumbled loudly, and the man laughed, and everything felt like it was going to be all right. They were safe. There were walls around them, and food was being put in front of them, and the watching eye of the bloody moon was far away, watching the scrubland instead of the sisters.

The men set their trays down in front of the sisters, whisking the silver domes away. In front of Jack, half a rabbit, roasted and served over an assortment of vegetables: plain food, peasant food, the sort of thing she might, given time, have learned to prepare for herself. There was a slice of bread and a square of cheese, and she had been raised to be polite, even when she didn't want to be; she did not complain about the strange shape of her meat, or the rough skins of the vegetables, which had been cooked perfectly, but in a more rustic manner than she was accustomed to.

In front of Jill, three slices of red roast beef, so rare that it was bleeding into the mashed potatoes and the spinach that surrounded it. No bread, no cheese, but a silver goblet full of fresh milk. The metal was covered in fine drops of condensation, like dew.

"Please," said the man. "Eat." Mary reached over and took the silver dome from his food, revealing a plate that looked very much like Jill's. His goblet matched hers as well, although the contents were darker; wine, perhaps. It looked like the wine their father sometimes drank with dinner.

Jack hoped that it was wine.

Jill began to eat immediately, falling on her food like a starving thing. She might have wrinkled her nose at meat that rare at home, but she hadn't eaten in more than a day; she would have eaten meat raw if it meant that she was eating *something*. Jack wanted to be more cautious. She wanted to see whether this stranger drugged her sister, or something worse, before she let her guard down. But she was so hungry, and the food smelled so good, and the man had said they'd be safe in his house for three days. Everything was strange, and they still didn't know his name—

She stopped in the act of reaching for her fork, turning to look at him with wide eyes while she frantically tried to kick Jill under the table. Her legs were too short and the table was too wide; she missed by more than a foot. "We don't know your name," she said, voice a little shrill. "That means you're a stranger. We're not even supposed to *talk* to strangers."

Mary paled, which Jack would have thought was impossible; the woman had almost no color in her to start with. The two silent servers took a step backward, putting their backs to the wall. And the man, the strange, nameless man in his red-lined cloak, looked amused.

"You don't know my name because you haven't earned it, little foundling," he said. "Most call me 'Master,' here. You may call me the same."

Jack stared at him and held her tongue, unsure of what she could possibly say; unsure of what would be *safe* to say. It was plain as the moon in the sky that the people who worked for this man were afraid of him. She just didn't know why, and until she knew why, she didn't want to say anything at all.

"You should eat," said the man, not unkindly. "Unless you'd prefer what your sister is having?"

Jack mutely shook her head. Jill, who had been eating throughout the exchange, continued to shovel meat and potato and spinach into her mouth, seemingly content with the world.

Heavy footsteps echoed up the stairs, loudly enough to catch the attention of everyone at the table, even Jill, who chewed and swallowed as she turned to look toward the sound. The man grimaced, an expression of distaste which only deepened as another stranger walked into the room.

This man was solid, built like a windmill, sturdy and strong and aching to burn. His clothing was practical, denim trousers and a homespun shirt, both protected by a leather apron. He had a chin that could have been used to split logs, and bright, assessing eyes below the heavy slope of his brow. Most fascinating of all was the scar that ran all the way along the circumference of his neck, heavy and white and frayed like a piece of twine, like whatever had cut him had made no effort whatsoever to do it cleanly.

"Dr. Bleak," said the first man, and sneered. "I wasn't sure you would deign to come. Certainly not so quickly. Don't you have some act of terrible butchery to commit?"

"Always," said Dr. Bleak. His voice was a rumble of thunder in the distant mountains, and Jack loved it at once. He sounded like a man who had shouted his way into understanding the universe. "But we had an arrangement, you and I. Or have you forgotten?"

The first man grimaced. "I sent for you, didn't I? I told Ivan to tell you that I remembered."

"The things Ivan says and the things you say are sometimes dissimilar." Dr. Bleak finally turned to look at Jack and Jill.

Jill had stopped eating. Both of them were sitting very, very still.

Dr. Bleak frowned at the red-stained potatoes on Jill's plate. The meat was long since gone, but the signs of it remained. "I see you've already made your choice," he said. "*That* was not a part of the arrangement."

"I allowed the girls to select their own meals," said the first man, sounding affronted. "It's not my fault if she prefers her meat rare."

"Mmm," said Dr. Bleak noncommittally. He

focused on Jill. "What's your name, child? Don't be afraid. I'm not here to harm you."

"Jillian," whispered Jill, in a squeak of a voice.

"Dr. Bleak lives outside the village," said the first man. "He has a hovel. Rats and spiders and the like. It's nothing compared to a castle."

Dr. Bleak rolled his eyes. "Really? *Really?* You're going to resort to petty insults? I haven't even made my choice yet."

"But as you're clearly going for the one I'd be inclined to favor, I feel no shame in pleading my case," said the first man. "Besides, *look* at them. A matched set! How could you begrudge me the desire to keep them both?"

"Wait," said Jack. "What do you mean, 'keep' us? We're not stray dogs. We're very sorry we trespassed in your big creepy field, but we're not *staying* here. As soon as we find a door, we're going home."

The first man smirked. Dr. Bleak actually looked . . . well, almost sad.

"The doors appear when they will," he said. "You could be here for a very long time."

Jack and Jill bore identical expressions of alarm. Jill spoke first.

"I have soccer practice," she said. "I can't miss it. They'll cut me from the team, and then Daddy will be furious with me."

"I'm not supposed to go outside," said Jack. "My mother's going to be so mad when she finds out that I did. We can't be here for a very long time. We just *can't*."

"But you will," said the first man. "For three days as guests in my home, and then as treasured residents, for as long as it takes to find a door back to your world. If you ever do. Not all foundlings return to the places that they ran away from, do they, Mary?"

"No, m'lord," said Mary, in a dull, dead voice.

"The last foundling to come stumbling into the Moors was a boy with hair like fire and eyes like a winter morning," said the first man. "Dr. Bleak and I argued over who should have his care and feeding—because we both love children, you see. They're so lively, so energetic. They can make a house feel like a home. In the end, I won, and I promised Dr. Bleak that, in order to keep the peace, he would have the next foundling to pass through. Imagine my surprise when there were two of you! Truly the Moon provides."

"Where is he now?" asked Jack warily.

"He found his door home," said Dr. Bleak. "He took it." He glared down the length of the table at the first man, like he was daring him to say something.

Instead, the first man simply laughed, shaking his head. "So dramatic! Always so dramatic. Sit down, Michel. Let me feed you. Enjoy the hospitality of my home for an evening, and perhaps you'll see the wisdom of letting these pretty sisters stay together."

"If you're so set on keeping them as a matched set, honor the spirit of our agreement and let them both come home with me," said Dr. Bleak. His next words were directed at the girls. "I can't keep you in luxury. I have no servants, and you'll be expected to work for your keep. But I'll teach you how the world works, and you'll go home wiser, if wearier. You will never be intentionally harmed beneath my roof."

The word "never" seemed to leap out at Jack. The first man had only promised them three days. She looked across the table at Jill and found her sister sulky-eyed and pouting.

"Will you eat, Michel?" asked the first man.

"I suppose I should," said Dr. Bleak, and dropped himself into a chair like an avalanche coming finally to rest. He looked to Mary. His eyes were kind. "Meat and bread and beer, if you would be so kind, Mary."

"Yes, sir," said Mary, and actually smiled as she fled the room.

The first man—the Master—raised his goblet in a mocking toast. "To the future," he said. "It's on its way now, whether we're prepared or not."

"I suppose that's true," said Dr. Bleak, to him, and "Eat," he said, to Jack and Jill. "You'll need your strength for what's to come.

"We all will."

6 THE FIRST NIGHT OF SAFETY

Jack and Jill were tucked away in the same round tower room, in two small beds shaped like teardrops, with their heads at the widest point and their feet pointed toward the tapering end. The windows were barred. The door was locked. "For your protection," Mary had said, before turning the key and sealing them in for the evening.

Many children would have railed at their confinement, would have gone looking for clever ways to pull the bars from the windows or break the latch on the door. Many children had been raised to believe that they were allowed to rail against unnecessary rules, that getting out of bed to use the bathroom or get a glass of water was not only allowed but encouraged, since taking care of their needs was more important than an eight-hour stretch spent perfectly in bed. Not Jack and Jill. They had been raised to obey, to behave, and so they stayed where they were.

(It is, perhaps, important to note that while blindly following rules can be a dangerous habit, it can also mean salvation. The ground below the tower window was white with old bones from children who had tried to make clever ropes out of braided sheets, only to find them too short and fall to their deaths. Some rules exist to preserve life.)

"We can't stay here," whispered Jack.

"We have to stay *somewhere*," whispered Jill. "If we have to wait for a door, why not wait here? It's nice here. I like it."

"That man wants us to call him *'master.'*"

"The other man wants us to call him 'doctor.' How is that different?"

Jack didn't know how to explain that those things were different; she just knew that they were, that one was a title that *said* something about the person who used it, while the other said how much that person knew, how much they understood about the world. One was a threat and the other was a reassurance.

"It just is," she said finally. "I want to go with Dr. Bleak. If we have to go with somebody, I want it to be him."

"Well, *I* want to stay here," said Jill. She scowled at her sister across the gap between their beds. "I don't see why we always have to do what you want to do."

There had never in their lives been a time when Jack was allowed to decide their actions. Their parents had always set the course for them, even down to their school days, where they had played out the roles set for them with the fervency of actors who knew the show would be cancelled if they made a single mistake. Jack was silent, stung, wondering how her sister could have read the world so very wrong.

Finally, in a soft voice, she said, "We don't have to stay together."

Jill had been enjoying spending time with her sister. It was . . . nice. It was nice to feel like they were together, like they were united, like they actually *agreed* on something. But she liked it there, in the big, fancy castle with the silver plates and the smiling man in the long black cloak. She liked feeling like she was safe behind thick walls, where that big red moon couldn't get her. She would have been happy to share being there with Jack, but she wasn't going to give it up because her sister liked some smelly, dirty doctor better.

"No, we don't," she said, and rolled over, and pretended to go to sleep.

Jack rolled onto her back and stared at the ceiling, and didn't pretend anything at all.

They were both tired, confused children with full stomachs, tucked into warm beds. Eventually, they both fell asleep, dreaming tangled dreams until the sound of the door being unbolted woke them. They sat up, still in the same dirty, increasingly tattered clothing they'd been wearing since their adventure began, and watched as the door swung open. Mary held it for the two men who had served them dinner the night before. Each carried a tray, setting them down next to the girls before whisking the lids away to reveal scrambled eggs, buttered toast, and slices of thick, greasy ham.

"The Master expects you to eat quickly," said Mary, as the men retreated to stand behind her. "He understands that you are in no position to clean yourselves up, and will forgive you for your untidiness. I'll wait in the hall until you're done and ready to see him."

"Wait," said Jack, feeling suddenly grimy and uncomfortable. She had almost forgotten how filthy she was. "Can we have a bath?"

"Not yet," said Mary, stepping out of the room. Again, the two men followed her; the last one out shut the door behind himself.

"Why can't we have a bath?" asked Jack plaintively.

"I don't need a bath," said Jill, who very much did. She grabbed her knife and fork, beginning to cut her ham into small squares.

Jack, who had never in her life been allowed to stay dirty for more than a few minutes, shuddered. She looked at her food, and saw only butter, grease, and other things that would add to the mess she was already wearing. She slid out of the bed, leaving the food where it was.

Jill frowned. "Aren't you going to eat?"

"I'm not hungry."

"*I'm* going to eat."

"That's okay. I can wait."

"Well, you shouldn't." Jill pointed to the door. "Tell Mary you're done, and maybe she'll let you get a bath. Or she'll let you talk to your new doctor friend. You'd like that, wouldn't you?"

"I'd like the bath more," said Jack. "You're sure you don't mind?"

"I'm going to steal all your toast," said Jill serenely, and Jack realized two very important things: first, that her sister still thought this was an adventure, something that would only last until she was tired of it and would then go mercifully away, and second, that she needed to leave as soon as possible. The Master—how she hated that she was starting to think of him that way!—struck her as the sort of person who wanted little girls to be decorative and pretty, toys lined up on a shelf. He hadn't talked about keeping them together because sisters needed to be together; he'd talked about keeping them together so he'd have a matching set.

If she couldn't get Jill out of there, she couldn't stay, because if she stayed, she would be better at being decorative. She would show Jill up. They wouldn't match, no matter how much they tried. And the Master . . .

She didn't know how she knew, but she knew that he wouldn't like that. He would be displeased. She didn't think either she or Jill would enjoy his displeasure.

Her dress was stiff and her tights stuck to her legs like bandages as she stepped out into the hall. Mary was waiting there, as she had promised, along with the two serving men.

"All done?" she asked.

Jack nodded. "Jill's still eating," she said. "I can wait here with you until she's done."

"No need," said Mary. "The Master doesn't care for dawdling. If you want him to choose you, you'd be well served by heading down now."

"What if I don't want him to choose me?"

Mary paused. She looked at the two dead-eyed men, assessing. Then she looked around the hall as a whole, seeming to search every crack and corner. Finally, when she was sure that they were alone, she returned her attention to Jack.

"If you don't want to be chosen, you run, girl. You go down to that throne room—"

"Throne room?" squeaked Jack.

"—and you tell Dr. Bleak you want to go with him, and you *run*. The Master likes your sister's appetite, but he likes the way you hold yourself. He likes the way you sit. He'll toy with her until the three days are up, and then he'll choose you and break her heart. He'll say that Dr. Bleak could leave you both here, but he knows Dr. Bleak would never do that. When he can save a foundling, he does. I wish to God that he'd saved me." There was fire in Mary's eyes, bright and burning like a candle. "Your sister will be safer if you're gone. He'll have to make her into a lady before he can make her into a daughter, and who knows? You may find your door before that happens."

"Were you . . ." Jack stopped, unsure of how to finish the question.

Mary nodded. "I was. But I never wanted to be his child, and when he asked me to let him be my father, I said no. So he kept me as a reminder to other foundlings that there are more places in a noble household than the ones set at the head of the table. He'll never harm her without her invitation: you don't need to worry about that. Men like him, they can't come in unless you invite them. You'll have time."

"Time for what?"

"Time to figure out why you were called to the Moors; time to decide whether or not you want to stay." Mary straightened, the fire seeming to go out as she turned to the nearest of the dead-eyed men. "Take her down to see the Master. Go quickly now. You'll need to be back up here before the second child is ready to descend."

The man nodded but did not speak. He beckoned for Jack to follow him, and he started down the stairs. Jack looked at Mary. Mary shook her head and said nothing. The time for words between them was done, it seemed; what Jack did from here was up to her. Jack hesitated. Jack looked at the door to the room where her sister sat, enjoying her breakfast.

Jack went down the stairs.

The dead-eyed man had predicted her recalcitrance; he was waiting on the first landing, as silent and impassive as ever. When she reached him, he started walking again, leaving her to trail along behind. His stride was long enough to force her to hurry, until it felt as if her feet were barely touching the ground, like she was going to tumble down the stairs and land at the bottom in a heap.

But that didn't happen. They reached the bottom and stepped back into the grand dining hall. The Master and Dr. Bleak were seated at opposite ends of the table, watching each other warily. Dr. Bleak had a plate of food in front of him, which he was not touching. The Master had another goblet of thick red wine. The dead-eyed man walked silently. Jack did not, and the Master and Dr. Bleak turned toward the sound of her arrival.

The Master looked at the stains on her dress, the tangles in her hair, and smiled. "So eager," he said, voice practically a purr. "Have you made your choice, then? It's clear you want first pick of guardians." *It's clear you're choosing me,* said the silence that followed.

"I have," said Jack. She stood as straight as she

could, trying not to let her shoulders shake or her knees knock. The choice had seemed difficult when she was alone with her sister. Now, with both men looking at her, it felt impossible.

Still, her feet moved, somehow, and carried her down the length of the room to stand next to a startled Dr. Bleak.

"I'd like to come and work for you, please," she said. "I'd like to learn."

Dr. Bleak looked at her soft hands and her frilly, lacy dress, and frowned. "It won't be easy," he said. "The work will be hard. You'll blister, and bleed, and leave something of yourself behind if you ever leave me."

"You told us that last night," said Jack.

"I don't have time for fripperies or finery. If you want those things, you should stay here."

Jack frowned, eyes narrowing. "Last night you wanted us both, even if you wanted my sister more," she said. "Now you seem like you don't want me at all. Why?"

Dr. Bleak opened his mouth to answer. Then he stopped, and cocked his head to the side, and said, "Honestly, I don't know. A willing apprentice is always better than an unwilling one. Shall I return for you in two days?"

"I'd rather go with you today," said Jack. She had a feeling that if she lingered, she would never leave, and again, that would go poorly for her sister—Jill, who had always been the strong one, always been the smart one, but who had never been expected to be the *clever* one. Jill trusted too easily, and got hurt even easier.

Jack had to go *now*.

If Dr. Bleak was surprised, he didn't show it. He simply nodded, said, "As you like," and stood, offering a shallow bow to the Master. "Thank you for honoring our agreement. As mine has chosen me, the second constitutes your turn; the next foundling to enter the Moors is mine by right."

"As yours has chosen you, and slighted me, what's to stop me killing her where she stands?" The Master sounded bored. That didn't stop the fear from coiling through Jack's heart, where it lay, heavy and waiting, like a serpent preparing to strike. "She forsook the protection of my house when she rejected me."

"She's more useful alive," said Dr. Bleak. "She's her sister's mirror. If something should . . . happen, to the first, you could draw upon the second to guarantee her survival. And if you killed her, you would break our bargain. Do you really want to risk a fight between us? Do you think this is the time?"

The Master scowled but did not rise. "As you like, Michel," he said, sounding almost bored. His eyes went to Jack, as calm as if he hadn't just threatened her. "If you tire of living in squalor, little girl, feel free to return. My doors are always open to one as lovely as you."

Jack, who had long since tired of being viewed as simply "lovely," and who had not forgotten the threat, even if the Master had, said nothing. She nodded, and stepped a little closer to Dr. Bleak, and when he rose and walked out of the room, she followed him.

But that is enough of Jack for now: this is a story about two children, even if it is sometimes necessary to follow one at the exclusion of the other. That is often the way. Give children the opportunity and they will scatter, forcing choices to be made, forcing the one who seeks them to run down all manner of dark corridors. And so:

Jill ate her breakfast, and when she was done, she ate Jack's breakfast, glaring all the while at her sister's empty bed. Stupid Jack. They were finally in a place where someone *liked* their shared face, their shared reflection, and now Jack was just going to walk away and leave her. She should have known that Jack wouldn't want to start being a twin now. Not when she'd spent so many years avoiding it.

(It did not occur to Jill that Jack's avoidance, like her own, had been born purely of parental desire and never of a sincere wanting. Their parents had done everything they could to blur the lines of twinhood, leaving Jack and Jill stuck in the middle. But Jack was gone and Jill was not, and in the moment, that was all that mattered.)

When the last scrap of toast had been used to mop up the last smear of egg, Jill finally got out of bed and walked to the door. Mary was waiting there, and she curtseyed when Jill emerged.

"Miss," she said. "Was breakfast to your liking?"

Jill, who had never been treated like she *mattered* before—especially not by an adult—beamed. "It was fine," she said grandly. "Did you see to my sister?"

"I'm sorry, miss, I believe she's already gone with Dr. Bleak. He doesn't often stay away from his laboratory long."

Jill's face fell. "Oh," she said. Until that moment, she hadn't realized how much she was hoping Jack would have changed her mind; would be waiting, penitent and hungry, on the stairs.

Let Jack throw away the chance to be a princess and live in a castle. Jack already knew what it was to be treated like royalty, to have the pretty dress and the shining tiara and the love of everyone around her. She'd realize her mistake and come crawling back, and would Jill forgive her?

Probably. It would be nice, to share this adventure with her sister.

"The Master is waiting, miss," said Mary. "Are you ready to see him?"

"Yes," said Jill, and *no* said something deep

inside her, a still, small voice that understood the danger they were in, even if that danger was shadowy and ill defined. Jill stood up a little straighter, raised her chin the way she'd seen Jack do when she was showing off a new dress to their mother's friends, and swallowed the fear as deep as it would go. "I want to tell him that I'll stay."

"You haven't a choice now, miss," said Mary. Her tone was cautioning, almost apologetic. "Once your sister chose to go, you were set to stay."

Jill frowned, the still, small voice that had been counseling caution instantly silenced in the face of this new affront. "Because *she* chose, I don't get to?"

"Yes, miss. I don't mean to speak out of turn, but you may wish to approach the Master with deference. He doesn't like being selected second."

Neither did Jill, and she had been selected second all her life. In that instant, hot, fierce love for the nameless man in the lonely castle washed over her, wiping any remnants of caution away. The Master was second-best for no good reason, just like she was. Well, she would make him understand that it wasn't true. She'd chosen him before Jack had even known her stupid Dr. Bleak existed. They were going to be happy together until the door home opened, and they were never going to be second-best again. Never.

"I chose him first. Jacqueline skipped breakfast so she could look like the star," said Jill, all bitterness and cold anger. "I'll tell him so."

Mary had seen many foundlings come and go since her own arrival in the Moors. She looked at Jill, and for the first time, she felt as if, perhaps, the Master might be pleased. This one might live long enough to leave, assuming the door home ever opened at all.

"Follow me, miss," she said, and turned, and walked down the stairs to where the Master waited, still and silent as he always was when he saw no need for motion.

(How the children who tumbled through the occasional doors between the Moors and elsewhere couldn't see that he was a predator, she didn't understand. Mary had known him for a predator the second she'd seen him. It had been a familiar danger: the family she had been fleeing from had been equally predatory, even if their predations had been of a more mundane nature. She had been comfortable in his care because she had known him, and when he had revealed himself fully to her, it had come as no surprise. That was rare. Most of the children she walked through these halls were terribly, terribly surprised when their time came, no matter how often they'd been warned. There would never be warning enough.)

The Master was sitting at the table when they

stepped back into the dining hall, sipping moodily from a silver goblet. He looked at Mary—and hence, at Jill—with narrow, disinterested eyes. He lowered his drink.

"I suppose we're stuck together," he said, looking at Jill.

"I chose you," said Jill.

The Master lifted his eyebrows. "Did you, now? I don't remember seeing you in front of me before your foolish sister left with that filthy doctor. I seem to recall sitting here alone, no foundling by my side, as she came down those stairs and declared her intent to go with him."

"She said she didn't want to stay," said Jill. "I thought it would be better if I ate my breakfast and let her go. That way, I'd be ready for whatever you wanted me to do today. Skipping meals isn't healthy."

"No, it's not," said the Master, with a flicker of what might have been amusement. "You swear you chose me before she chose him?"

"I chose you as soon as I saw you," said Jill earnestly.

"I don't care for liars."

"I don't lie."

The Master tilted his head, looking at her with new eyes. Finally, he said, "You will need to be washed and dressed, prepared to live here with me. My household has certain standards. Mary will assist you in meeting them. You will be expected to present yourself when I want you, and to otherwise stay out from underfoot. I will arrange for tutors and for tailors; you will want for nothing. All I ask in exchange are your loyalty, your devotion, and your obedience."

"Unless her door comes," said Mary.

The Master shot a sharp, narrow-eyed glance in her direction. She stood straight and met his eyes without flinching. In the end, astonishingly, it was the Master who looked away.

"You will always be free to take the door back to your original home," he said. "I am bound by a compact as old as the Moors to let you go, if that's truly your desire. But I hope that when that door eventually opens, you might find that you prefer my company."

Jill smiled. The Master smiled back, and his teeth were very sharp, and very white.

Both girls, through different routes, down different roads, had come home.

7 TO FETCH
A PAIL OF WATER

Dr. Bleak lived outside the castle, outside the village; outside the seemingly safe bulk of the wall. The gates opened when he approached them, and he strode through, never looking back to see whether Jack was following him. She was—of course she was—but her life had been defined by sitting quietly and being decorative, allowing interesting things to come to her, rather than chasing them through bracken and briar. Her chest felt like it was too tight. Her heart thudded and her side ached, making speech impossible.

Once, only once, she stumbled to a stop and stood, swaying, eyes fixed on her feet as she tried to get her breath back. Dr. Bleak continued onward for a few more steps before he stopped in turn. Still, he did not look back.

"You are not Eurydice, but I won't risk losing you to something so trivial," he said. "You need to be stronger."

Jack, who could not breathe, said nothing.

"We'll have time to improve what can be improved, and compensate for what can't," he said. "But night comes quickly here. Recover, and resume."

Jack took a vast, shaky breath, following it with a step, and then with another. Dr. Bleak waited until he heard her take the third step. Then he resumed his forward progress, trusting Jack to keep pace.

She did. Of course she did. There was no other choice remaining. And if she thought longingly of the soft bed where she'd spent the night, or the comfortable dining hall where the Master had served them delicate things on silver trays, well. She was twelve years old; she had never worked for anything in her life. It was only reasonable that she should yearn for something that felt like a close cousin to the familiar, even if she knew, all the way down to her bones, that she did not, should not, *would* not want it for her own.

Dr. Bleak led her through the bracken and brush, up the sloping side of a hill, until the shape of a windmill appeared in the distance. It seemed very close, and then, as they walked on and on without reaching it, she realized that it was, instead, very large; it was a windmill meant to harness the entire sky. Jack stared. Dr. Bleak walked, and she followed, until the brush under their feet gave way to a packed-earth trail, and they began the final ascent toward the windmill. The last part of the hill was steeper than the rest, ending some ten feet before the door. The ground all around the foundation had been cleared and covered in raised planter beds that grew green with plants Jack had never seen before.

"Touch nothing until you know what it is," said Dr. Bleak, not unkindly. "No honest question will go unanswered, but many of the things here are dangerous to the unprepared. Do you understand?"

"I think so," said Jack. "Can I ask a question now?"

"Yes."

"What did you mean before, about drawing on me to save Jill?"

"I meant blood, little girl. Everything comes down to blood here, one way or another. Do you understand?"

Jack hesitated before shaking her head.

"You will," said Dr. Bleak, and pulled a large iron key out of the pocket of his apron, and unlocked the windmill door.

The room on the other side was vast, large enough to seem cavernous, bounded on all sides by the curving windmill walls, and yet no less intimidating for its limitations. The ceiling was more than twenty feet overhead, covered with dangling things the likes of which Jack had never seen before: stuffed reptiles and birds and something that looked like a pterodactyl, leathery wings spread wide and frozen for eternity. Racks of tools and shelves laden with strange bottles and stranger implements lined the walls.

There was a large oaken table near the smallest of the room's three fireplaces, and what looked like a surgical table at the very center of the room, well away from any source of heat. There were unknowable machines, and jars filled with terrible biological specimens that seemed to track her with their lifeless eyes. Jack walked slowly into the very center of the room, where she could turn, taking everything in.

A spiral stairway occupied the center of the room, winding down into the basement and up into the heights of the structure, where there must be other rooms, other horrifying wonders. It seemed strange, that a windmill should have a basement. It was something she had never considered before.

Dr. Bleak watched her, the door still open behind him. If the girl was going to flee screaming into the night, it was going to happen now. He had been expecting the other one to come with him, the one with the short hair and the fingernails that had been worn down and dirtied by playing in the yard. He knew more than most that appearances could be deceiving, but he had found that certain markers were often true. This girl looked cosseted, sheltered; girls like her did not often thrive in places like this.

She stopped looking. She turned back to him. She plucked at the stained and increasingly stiff skirt of her dress.

"I think this will get caught on things," she said. "Is there something else that I could wear?"

Dr. Bleak lifted his eyebrows. "That's your only question?"

"I don't know what most of these things are, but you said you were going to teach me," said Jack. "I don't know what questions I'm supposed to *ask,* so I guess I'm going to let you give me the answers, and then I can match them up with the questions. I can't do that if I'm getting snagged on everything all the time."

Dr. Bleak gave her an assessing look, closing the door. Somehow, he no longer worried that she was going to run. "I warned you that you'd work if you came with me. I'll put calluses on your hands and bruises on your knees."

"I don't mind working," said Jack. "I haven't done it much, but I'm tired of sitting still."

"Very well." Dr. Bleak walked across the room to one of the high shelves. He reached up and lifted down a trunk, as lightly as if it were made of cobwebs and air. Setting it down on the floor, he said, "Take what you like. Everything is clean; nothing is ever put away here without being cleaned first."

Jack heard that for the instruction that it was, and nodded before walking carefully over to the trunk and kneeling to open it. It was full of clothing—children's clothing, some of it in styles she had never seen before. Much of it seemed old-fashioned, like something out of an old black-and-white movie. Some was made of shimmering, almost futuristic fabric, or cut to fit bodies she couldn't quite envision, torsos as long as legs, or with three arms, or with no hole for the head.

In the end, she selected a white cotton shirt with starched cuffs and collar, and a knee-length black skirt made of what felt like canvas. It would be sturdy enough to stand up to learning how to work, unlikely to snag or stop her in her tracks. The thought of wearing someone else's underthings was unsettling, no matter how many times they'd been bleached, but in the end, she also selected a pair of white shorts, her cheeks burning with the indignity of it all.

Dr. Bleak, who had watched her make her selections (all save for the shorts; when he'd realized what she was looking for, he had turned politely aside), did not smile; smiling was not his way. But he nodded approvingly, and said, "Up the stairs, you will find several empty rooms. One of them will be yours, to keep your things in, to use when you need to be alone. You will not have many opportunities for idleness. I suggest you enjoy them when you can."

Jack hesitated.

"Yes?" asked Dr. Bleak.

"I'm . . . it's not just my dress that's filthy," said Jack, grimacing a little, like she had never admitted to dirtiness in her life. Which perhaps she hadn't: perhaps she had never been given the opportunity. "Is there any chance I could have a bath?"

"You will have to haul the water yourself, and heat it, but if that is all you desire, yes." Dr. Bleak closed the trunk, lifting it back onto the shelf where it belonged. Then he took down a vast tin bucket from a hook that dangled from the ceiling. It was shallow enough that Jack thought she could crawl into it if she needed to, almost as large as the bathtub at home.

Her eyes widened. The bathtub at home. This and that were the same, separated by centuries of technological advancement, but serving an identical purpose.

Dr. Bleak set the bucket down in front of the largest of the three fires before lifting a kettle down from the shelf and handing it to Jack. "The well is outside," he said. "I will be back in two hours. Figure out how to clean yourself." Then he was gone, striding back to the door and stepping out onto the Moors, leaving Jack to gape after him, the kettle in her hands, utterly bemused.

"The Master wants you cleaned and smartened up," said Mary, dragging a brush through the tangled strands of Jill's hair. Jill ground her teeth, trying not to flinch away from the bristles. She was used to brushing her own hair, and sometimes she allowed knots to form for weeks, until they had to be cut out with scissors.

The room she'd been removed to was small and smelled of talcum powder and sharp copper. The walls were papered in the palest pink, and a vanity much like her mother's took up one entire wall. There was no mirror. That was the only truly odd thing about the room, which was otherwise queasily familiar to Jill, the sort of feminine stronghold that she had always been denied admission to. Her sister was the one who should have been sitting on this stool, having her hair brushed, ready to be "smartened up."

"It's a shame it's so short," said Mary, seemingly unaware of Jill's discomfort. "Ah, well. Hair will grow, and at least this way, he'll be able to decide what length he likes best without cutting off something that's already there."

"I get to grow my hair out?" asked Jill, suddenly hopeful.

"Long enough to cover your throat," said Mary, and her tone was dire, and Jill missed it entirely. She was too busy thinking of what she'd look like with long hair, how it would feel against the back of her neck; wondering whether adults on the street would smile at her the way they smiled at Jack, like she was something special, something *beautiful,* and not just another tomboy.

The trouble with denying children the freedom to be themselves—with forcing them into an idea of what they should be, not allowing them to choose their own paths—is that all too often, the one drawing the design knows nothing of the desires of their model. Children are not formless clay, to be shaped according to the sculptor's whim, nor are they blank but identical dolls, waiting to be slipped into the mode that suits them best. Give ten children a toy box, and watch them select ten different toys, regardless of gender or religion or parental expectations. Children have *preferences*. The danger comes when they, as with any human, are denied those preferences for too long.

Jill had always wanted to know what it was like to be allowed to wear her hair long, to put on a pretty skirt, to sit next to her sister and hear people cooing over what a lovely matched pair they were. She liked sports, yes, and she liked reading her books; she liked *knowing* things. She would probably have been a soccer player even if her father hadn't insisted, would definitely have watched spaceships on TV and superheroes in the movies, because the core of who *Jill* was had nothing to do with the desires of her parents and everything to do with the desires of her heart. But she would have done some of those things in a dress. Having half of everything she wanted denied to her for so long had left her vulnerable to them: they were the forbidden fruit, and like all forbidden things, even the promise of them was delicious.

"Your hair will take time," said Mary, seeing that her warnings had gone unheard. "Your clothing, we can fix right away—in time for your lunch. A bath has been drawn for you." She set the brush aside, motioning for Jill to get off the chair. "I'll have your new attire ready when you get out."

Jill stood, all eyes and anticipation. "Where do I go?"

"There," said Mary, and indicated a door that hadn't been there a moment before.

Jill hesitated. Doors were dangerous things. The Master (and that dreadful Dr. Bleak) had talked about doors that would take her home again, and she wasn't *ready* to go home. She wanted to stay here, to enjoy her adventure in a world where she was allowed to have long hair and wear skirts and be whoever she wanted to be.

Mary saw the hesitation and sighed, shaking her head. "This is not your doorway home," she said. "The Master's castle is malleable, and matches to our needs. Go. Clean yourself up. It doesn't do to keep him waiting."

Mary's warnings might have gone unnoticed, but Jill had grown up surrounded by adults who said one thing and did another, adults who were so consumed with *wanting* that it never occurred to them to wonder whether children might not know about wanting too. She knew better than to disappoint if she could help it.

"All right," she said, and opened the door, and stepped into a mermaid's grotto, into a drowned girl's sanctuary. The walls were tiled in glittering blue and silver, like scales, arching together to form the high, pointed dome of the roof. It was a flower frozen in the moment before it could open; it was a teardrop turned to crystal before it could fall. Little nooks were set into the walls, filled with candles, which cast a dancing light over everything they touched.

The floor was a narrow lip, no more than two feet at its widest point, circling the outside of the room. The rest was given over to a basin filled with sweetly scented water, dotted with frothing mounds of bubbles. Everything smelled of roses and vanilla. Jill stopped and stared. This was . . . this was amazing, this was incredible, and it was *all for her.*

A small dart of smug delight wedged itself in her heart. Jack wasn't here. Jack wasn't standing in this room, looking at a bath fit for a fairy tale princess. This was hers, and hers alone. She was the princess in this story.

(Would she have felt bad about her smugness if she had known that, at that very moment, Jack was puzzling her way through the process of getting water from well to kettle to tin tub without scalding or freezing herself? Or would it have delighted her to think of her poised and pampered sister sitting in lukewarm water to her hips, marinating in her own dirt, scrubbing the worst of it away with brittle yellow sponges that had once been living things, and were now remembered only by their bones? How quickly they grow apart, when there is something to be superior about.)

Jill removed her stained and filthy clothing and stepped into the bath. The temperature was perfect, and the water was silky-smooth with perfumes and oils. She sank down to her chin and closed her eyes, enjoying the heat, enjoying the feeling that soon, she would be *clean*.

Some untold time later, there was a knock at the door, and Mary's voice said, briskly, "Time to come out, miss. Your clothes are ready, and it's nearly time for lunch."

Jill snapped out of her daze, opening her mouth to protest—it couldn't be time for lunch, they'd just eaten breakfast—before her stomach gave a loud growl. The water was still warm, but maybe that didn't matter in a magic room inside a magic castle.

"Coming!" she called, and waded through the water toward the place where she'd left her clothes. They were gone, a towel and robe in their place. Understanding what was expected of her, Jill dried her body with the towel and covered it with the robe, which was soft and white and felt almost like the bubbles from her bath. There was no towel rack or hamper. She folded the used towel as carefully as she could and put it down against the base of the wall, hoping that would be tidy enough, *good* enough, for her host. Then she let herself out of the room, to where Mary waited.

The maid gave her a thoughtful once-over before saying, in a faintly surprised tone, "I suppose you'll do. Here." She picked up a bundle of pale fabric—purple and blue and white, like a bruise in the process of healing—and thrust it at the girl. "Get dressed. If you need help with the buttons, I'll be here. The Master is waiting."

Jill nodded silently as she took the clothes, and was unsurprised to see that a screen had appeared on the far side of the room. She slipped behind it, setting the clothes down on the waiting stool before untying her robe and beginning to dress herself.

She was relieved to find that the undergarments were ones she recognized, panties and a slip-chemise that was halfway to being a thin tank top. The dress, though . . . oh, the dress.

It was an ocean of cascading silk, a sea of draped fabric. It was not an adult dress, meant to grace an adult figure; it was a fantasy gown intended for a child, one that made her look as much like an inverted orchid as she did a girl. It took her three tries to figure out which hole was for her head and which were for her arms, and when she was done, the whole thing seemed to slouch around her, unwilling to fit properly.

"Mary?" she said, hopefully.

The maid appeared around the corner of the screen, clucking her tongue when she saw the state Jill was in. "You have to fasten it if you want it to fit you," she said, and began doing up buttons and ties and snaps, so many that Jill's head spun just watching Mary's fingers move.

But when Mary was done, the dress fit Jill like it had been tailored for her. Looking down, Jill could see her bare toes peeping out from beneath the cascading skirts, and she was grateful, because without that one small flaw, it would have all been too perfect to be real. She looked up. Mary was holding a purple choker with a small pearl-and-amethyst pendant dangling from its center. Her expression was grave.

"You are a member of the Master's household now," she said. "You must always, always wear your choker when you're in the company of anyone other than the servants. That includes the Master. Do you understand me?"

"Why?" asked Jill.

Mary shook her head. "You'll understand soon enough," she said. Leaning forward, she tied the choker around Jill's neck. It was tight, but not so tight as to be uncomfortable; Jill thought she would be able to get used to it. And it was beautiful. She didn't get to wear beautiful things very often.

"There," said Mary, stepping back and looking

at her frankly. "You're as good as you're going to get without more time, and time's a thing we don't have right now. You're to sit quietly. Speak when spoken to. Think before you agree to anything. Do you understand?"

No, Jill thought, and "Yes," Jill said, and that was that: there was no saving her.

Mary, who had not spoken the word "vampire" aloud in over twenty years, who knew all too well the limitations that they labored under, only sighed and offered her hand to the girl. "All right," she said. "It's time."

When Dr. Bleak returned from his errands with an armful of firewood and a bundle of herbs, it was to find Jack in the front yard, carefully wiping the last of the grime from the sides of the tin tub. She looked up at the sound of his footsteps. He stopped where he was and looked at her like he was seeing her for the first time.

It had taken her six trips to the well and three turns with the kettle, but she had washed the grime from her body and hair, using a thick, caustic soap that she'd found next to the sponges. Her hair was braided sensibly back, and the only things that remained of her old attire were her shoes, patent leather and wiped as clean as the rest of her. She still looked too delicate to be a proper lab assistant, but appearances can be deceiving, and she had not balked from what he'd asked of her.

"What's for dinner?" asked Dr. Bleak.

"I have no idea, and you wouldn't want to eat it if I did," said Jack. "I don't know how to cook. But I'm willing to learn."

"Willing to learn, but not to lie?"

Jack shrugged. "You would have caught me."

"I suppose that's true," said Dr. Bleak. "Are you truly willing to learn?"

Jack nodded.

"All right, then," said Dr. Bleak. "Come inside." He walked across the yard with great, ground-eating steps, and when he stepped through the open door, Jack followed without hesitation.

She closed the door behind herself.

PART III

JACK AND JILL
WITH TIME TO KILL

8 THE SKIES TO SHAKE, THE STONES TO BLEED

It would become quickly dull, recounting every moment, every hour the two girls spent, one in the castle and one in the windmill, one in riches and one in artfully mended rags: it would become quickly dull, and so it shall not be our focus, for we are not here for dullness, are we? No. We are here for a story, whether it be wild adventure or cautionary tale, and we do not have the time to waste on mundane things. And yet.

And yet.

And yet look to the castle on the bluffs, the castle near to the sea, which sits atop a crumbling cliff in the belly of the lowlands. Look to the castle where the golden-haired girl walks the battlements at dusk and dawn in her dresses like dreams, with her throat concealed from prying eyes, with the wind tying beautiful knots in the long curtain of her hair. She waxes and wanes like the moon, now pale as milk, now healthy and pink as any village girl. There are those in the village below who whisper that she is the Master's daughter, sired on a princess from a far-away land and finally returned to her father when he howled her name to the western winds.

(There are those in the village who whisper darker things, who speak of disappearing children and lips stained red as roses. She is not a vampire yet, they say, and "yet" is such a powerful, unforgiving word that there is no questioning its truth, and no hiding from its promises.)

And yet look to the windmill in the hills, the windmill on the Moors, which stands higher than anything around it, inviting lightning, tempting disaster. Look to the windmill where the golden-haired girl works in the soil at all hours of the day and night, with her hands protected from the soil by heavy leather gloves and from everything else by gloves of the finest suede. She toils without cease, burns her sleeves on smoking machinery, strains her eyes peering into the finest workings of the universe. There are those in the village near the cliffs who smile to see her coming, dogging at the doctor's heels, her shoes becoming sturdier and more sensible with every passing season. She is learning, they say; she is finding her way.

(There are those in the village who whisper darker things, who point out the similarities between her and the Master's daughter, who recognize that a single body can only contain so much blood, can only take so much damage. She is not called to service yet, but when the Master and Dr. Bleak clash, there is never any question of the winner.)

Look at them, growing up, growing into the new shapes that have been offered to them, growing into girls their parents would not recognize, would turn their noses up at. Look at them finding themselves in this wind-racked place, where even the moon is not always safe to look upon.

Look at them in their solitary beds, in their solitary lives, growing further and further apart from one another, unable to entirely let go. Look at the girl in the gossamer gowns standing on the battlements, yearning for a glimpse of her sister; look at the girl in the dirty apron sitting atop the windmill, looking toward the distant walls of the town. They have so much, and so little, in common.

Someone with sharp enough eyes might see the instant where one wounded heart begins to rot while the other starts to heal. Time marches on.

There are moments in the years that we are skipping over, moments that are stories in and of themselves. Jack and Jill begin their menses on the same day (a word that comes from the village women and from Mary, who came from a different time, and Jack finds it charming in its antiquity, and Jill finds it terrifying in its strangeness). Jack packs her underpants with rags and begins trying to find a better way. It is unsafe, on the Moors, to smell of blood. Dr. Bleak calls the village women to help her. They bring their old clothes and their sewing needles; she rampages through his herbs and simples, testing chemical combinations until she strikes upon the right one. Together, she and the village women make something stronger and safer, which holds the smell of blood from prying noses. It keeps them safe when they have cause to venture out of their homes. It keeps monsters and the Master from noticing them.

They learn to love her, at least a little, on that day.

While all this is happening, Jill sinks deeper and deeper into her perfumed baths, bleeding into the water, emerging only to eat plates of chopped beef and spinach, her head spinning with the strangeness of it all. And when her period passes, the Master comes to her, and finally shows her his teeth, which she has been dreaming of for so long. He talks to her all night, almost until the sunrise, making sure that she's comfortable, making sure she *understands*.

He is not so different from the boys she had been dreading meeting when she started her high school career. Like them, he wants her for her body. Like them, he is bigger than her, stronger than her, more powerful than her in a thousand ways. But unlike them, he tells her no lies, puts no veils before his intentions; he is hungry, and she is meat for his table, she is wine for his cup. He promises to love her until the stars burn out. He promises to make her like him, when she is old enough, so that she will never need to leave the Moors. And when he asks her for her answer, she unties the choker that has circled her neck for the last two years, lets it fall away, and exposes the soft white curve of her neck.

There are moments that change everything.

A year after Jill becomes the Master's child in everything but name, Jack stands next to Dr. Bleak on the top floor of their shared windmill. The roof has been opened, and the storm that stains the sky is black as ink, writhing and lit from within by flashes of lightning. A village girl lies stretched on the stone slab between them, her body covered by a sheet, her hands strapped tight around two metal rods. She is only a year older than Jack, found dead when the sun rose, with a streak of white in her hair that spoke to a heart stopped when some phantom lover kissed her too deeply. Hearts that have been stopped without being damaged can sometimes start again, under the right circumstances. When the right circumstances cannot be arranged, lightning can make a surprisingly good substitute.

Dr. Bleak howls orders and Jack hurries to fulfill them, until lightning snakes down from the sky and strikes their array of clever machines. Jack is thrown across the room by the impact; she will taste pennies in the back of her throat for three days. Everything is silence.

The girl on the slab opens her eyes.

There are moments that change everything, mired in the mass of more ordinary time like insects caught in amber. Without them, life would be a tame, predictable thing. But with them, ah. With them, life does as it will, like lightning, like the wind that blows across the castle battlements, and none may stop it, and none may tell it "no." Jack helps the girl off the slab, and everything is different, and nothing will ever be the same.

The girl has eyes as blue as the heather that grows on the hill, and her hair, where it is not white, is the golden color of drying bracken, and she is beautiful in ways Jack fumbles to find the words for, ways that seem to defy the laws of nature and the laws of science in the same breath. Her name is Alexis, and it is a crime that she was ever dead, even for a second, because the world is darker when she's gone.

(Jack hadn't noticed the darkness, but that doesn't matter. A man who has lived his entire life in a cave does not mourn the sun until he sees it, and once he has, he can never go back underground.)

When Alexis kisses her for the first time, out behind the windmill, Jack realizes that she and Jill have one thing in common: she never, *never* wants to go back to the world she came from. Not when she could have this world, with its lightning and its blue-eyed, beautiful girls, instead.

There are moments that change everything,

and once things have been changed, they do not change back. The butterfly may never again become a caterpillar. The vampire's daughter, the mad scientist's apprentice, they will never again be the innocent, untouched children who wandered down a stairway, who went through a door.

They have been changed.

The story changes with them.

"Jack!" Dr. Bleak's voice was sharp, commanding, and impossible to ignore. Not that Jack was in the habit of ignoring it. Her first season with the doctor had been more than sufficient to teach her that when he said "jump," her correct response wasn't to ask "how high?" It was to run for the nearest cliff and trust that gravity would sort things out.

Still, sometimes he had the *worst* timing. She untangled herself from Alexis's arms, grabbing her gloves from the shelf where they had been discarded, and yanked them on while shouting, "Coming!"

Alexis sighed as she sat up and pulled her shift back into position. "What does he want *now?*" she asked. "Papa expects me back before nightfall." Days on the Moors were short, precious things. Sometimes the sun didn't come entirely out from behind the clouds for weeks at a time, allowing careful vampires and careless werewolves to run free even when it shouldn't have been their time. Alexis's family ran an inn. They didn't have to worry about farming or hunting during the scarce hours of daylight. That didn't mean they were in any hurry to offer their child a second funeral.

(Those who had died once and been resurrected couldn't become vampires: whatever strange mechanism the undead used to reproduce themselves was magic, and it shied away from the science of lightning and the wheel. Alexis was safe from the Master's whims, no matter how pretty she became as she aged. But the Master wasn't the only monster on the Moors, and most wouldn't care about Alexis's medical history. They would simply devour her.)

"I'll find out," said Jack, hastily buttoning her own vest. She stopped to look at Alexis, taking in the soft white curves of her body, the rounded flesh of her shoulder and breast. "Just . . . just stay right where you are, all right? I'll be back as soon as I can. If you don't move, we won't have to take another bath."

"I won't move," said Alexis, with a lazy smile, before lying back on the bed and staring at the taxidermy-studded ceiling.

After four years with Dr. Bleak, Jack had grown stronger than she ever could have expected, capable of hoisting dead bodies and bushels of potatoes over her shoulders with equal ease. She had grown like a weed, shooting up more than a foot, necessitating multiple trips to the village to buy new cloth to mend her trousers. The contents of Dr. Bleak's wardrobe trunk had stopped fitting her properly by the time she was fourteen, all long limbs and budding breasts and unpredictable temper. (Much of that year had been spent shouting at Dr. Bleak for reasons she could neither understand nor explain. To his credit, the doctor had borne up admirably under her unpredictable tempers. He was, after all, somewhat unpredictably tempered himself.)

After the third pair of badly patched trousers had split down the middle, Jack had learnt to tailor her own clothes, and had started buying fabric by the bolt, cutting and shaping it into the forms she desired. Her work was never going to make her the toast of some fashionable vampire's court, but it covered her limbs and provided her with the necessary protection from the elements. Dr. Bleak had nodded in quiet understanding as her attire became more and more like his, with cuffs that went to her wrists and buttoned tight, and cravats tied at her throat, seemingly for fashion but really to prevent anything getting past the fine weave of her armor. She was not denying her femininity by wearing men's clothing; rather, she was protecting it from caustic chemicals and other, less mundane compounds.

She was still thin, for while her belly was generally full, she did not have the luxury of second helpings or sweet puddings with her tea; she was still fair, for daylight was rare on the Moors. Her hair was still long, a tight blonde braid hanging down the center of her back, picked free and retied every morning. Alexis said that it was like butter, and sometimes cajoled Jack into letting her unbraid it so that she could run her fingers through the kinked strands, smoothing and soothing them. But it was never loose for long. Like everything else about Jack, it had grown into something precise and organized, always bent to its place in the world.

The newest things about her were her glasses, the lenses milled and shaped in Dr. Bleak's lab, set into bent-wire frames. Without them, the world was slightly fuzzy around the edges— not a terrible thing, given how brutal this world could sometimes be, but not the best of attributes in a scientist. So she wore her glasses, and she saw things as they were, sharp and bright and unforgiving.

She found Dr. Bleak inside the windmill, a large brown bat spread out on the autopsy table with nails driven through the soft webbing of its wings. Its mouth was stuffed full of garlic and wild rose petals, just as a precaution. There was nothing about the bat to *prove* that it was a visiting vampire, but there was nothing to prove that it *wasn't,* either.

"I need you to go to the village," he said, not

looking up. An elaborate loupe covered his left eye, bringing the internal organs of the bat into terrible magnification. "We're running low on aconite, arsenic, and chocolate biscuits."

"I still don't understand how we even have chocolate here," said Jack. "Cocoa trees grow in tropical climates. This is not a tropical climate."

"The terrible things that dwell beneath the bay scavenge it from the ships they wreck and trade it to the villagers for vodka," said Dr. Bleak. "That's also where we get rum, tea, and the occasional cursed idol."

"But where do the ships *come* from?"

"Far away." Dr. Bleak finally looked up, making no effort to conceal his irritation. "As you cannot dissect, resurrect, or otherwise scientifically trouble the sea, leave it *alone,* apprentice."

"Yes, sir," said Jack. The rest of Dr. Bleak's words finally caught up with her. Her eyes widened. "The village, sir?"

"Has your time with your buxom friend destroyed what little sense you had? I'm of no mood to take a new apprentice, not when you're finally becoming trained enough to be useful. Yes, Jack, the village. We need things. You are the apprentice. You fetch things."

"But sir . . ." Jack glanced to the window. The sun, such as it was, hung dangerously low in the sky. "Night is coming."

"Which is why you'll be purchasing aconite, to ward off werewolves. The gargoyles of the waste won't trouble you. They're still grateful for the repair job we did last month on their leader. As for vampires, well. You haven't much to worry about in that regard."

Jack wanted to argue. She opened her mouth to argue. Then she closed it again, recognizing a losing proposition when she saw one. "May I walk Alexis home?" she asked.

"As long as it doesn't make you late for the shops, I don't care what you do," said Dr. Bleak. "Give my regards to her family."

"Yes, sir," said Jack. Giving Dr. Bleak's regards to Alexis's family would probably mean coming home with a pot of stew and a loaf of bread, at the very least. They knew that he had given back their daughter, and more, they knew that Alexis was beautiful: her death and resurrection had probably protected her from an eternity of vampirism. For that alone, they would be grateful until the stars blew out.

Jack picked up the basket from beside the door, and counted out twenty small gold coins stamped with the Master's face from the jar that held their spending money. Then, shoulders slightly slumped, she went to tell Alexis that they were leaving.

Dr. Bleak waited until she was gone before he sighed, shaking his head, and reached for another scalpel. Jack was an excellent apprentice, eager to learn, obedient enough to be worth training, rebellious enough to be worth caring about. She would make a good doctor someday, if the Moors chose to keep her long enough. And that was the problem.

There were very few people born to the Moors. Alexis, with her calm native acceptance that this was the way the world was intended to work, was more of an aberration than a normalcy. Unlike some worlds, which maintained their own healthy populations, the Moors were too inimical to human life for that to be easily accomplished. So they sent doors to other places, to collect children who might be able to thrive there, and then they let what would happen naturally . . . happen.

Dr. Bleak had not been born to the Moors. Neither, truth be told, had the Master. The Master had been there for centuries; Dr. Bleak, for decades. Long enough to train under his own teacher, the bone-handed Dr. Ghast, who had trained under her own teacher, once upon a time. He knew that one day, he would die, and the lightning would not be enough to call him back. Some days, he thought he might even welcome that final period of rest, when he would no longer be called upon to play the lesser villain of the piece—who was, by comparison, the unwitting hero. He had not been born to the Moors, but he had been there for long enough to recognize the shape of things.

The Master had taken Jill as his latest daughter. She walked the battlements nightly, smiling and humming to herself; her regard for human life dwindled by the day. She was not yet a vampire, nor would be for several years, but it was . . . troubling . . . that a door should open and deposit two so well matched, yet so suited for opposing roles, into the Moors.

Did the Moon, all-seeing and all-judging, tire of the Master, as She had tired of so many vampire-lords before him? Jill would make a truly brutal replacement, once the last of her human softness was stripped away. Dr. Bleak could see the story stretching out from the moment of Jill's transformation. Jack, for all that she had little to do with her sister anymore, preferring to avoid the cloying glories of the Master's regard whenever possible, was still of the same blood. She wouldn't forgive the Master for taking her sister away from her. A determined mad scientist was a match for any monster—they were the human side of the essential balance between the feudal houses that ruled these shores—and he could easily see the Master destroyed, while his bright new child ascended, callous and cruel, to his throne.

Jack and Jill were a story becoming real in front of him, and he didn't know how to stop it. So yes, he was trying to force Jack to see her sister. He needed Jill to remember that Jack existed, that

138

Jack was human, and that logic said Jill must be human as well.

It might be the only thing that saved them.

Alexis sat up again when she heard Jack approach, and frowned at the expression on her face. "That doesn't look like 'everything's fixed, now kiss me more,'" she said.

"Because it's not," said Jack. "Dr. Bleak wants me to go into the village for supplies."

"Now?" Alexis made no effort to conceal her distress. "But I've only been here for an hour!" Which meant that—after the bath, and the physical exam, and the cleansing of her teeth, and the gargling with sharp, herbal disinfectant, to make sure that no bacteria had been knocked loose when she flossed—she had only been clean enough, by Jack's standards, for about five minutes before they'd been interrupted.

"I know," said Jack, kicking the floor in frustration. "I don't know why he's so set on my doing this now. I'm sorry. At least I can walk you home?"

Alexis heaved a put-upon sigh. "At least there's that," she agreed. "My mother will try to feed you dinner."

"Which I will gratefully accept, because your mother boils everything to within an inch of its life," said Jack. "If she asks why I don't remove my gloves, I'll tell her I've cut my hand and don't want to risk the wound cracking open, bleeding, and attracting the undead."

"That's what you told her last time."

"It's a valid concern. She should be pleased that you're stepping out with such a conscientious young apprentice, instead of one of those village oafs." Jack offered Alexis her gloved hand.

With another sigh, Alexis took it and slid off the bed. "Those 'village oafs,' as you like to call them, will have houses and trades of their own one day. You'll have a windmill."

"A very *clean* windmill," said Jack.

"They'd be able to give me children. That's what Mother says."

"I could give you children," said Jack, sounding faintly affronted. "You'd have to tell me how many heads you wanted them to have, and what species you'd like them to be, but what's the point of having all these graveyards if I can't give you children when you ask for them?"

Alexis laughed and punched her in the shoulder, and Jack smiled, knowing that all was forgiven.

They made an odd pair, strolling across the Moors, neither of them looking like they had a care in the world. Alexis was soft where Jack was spare, the daughter of wealthy parents who made sure she never went to bed hungry, trusting her to know her own body and its needs. (And if the local vampire favored willowy girls who would die if left outside in the slightest frost, well, loosen your belt and pass the potatoes; we'll keep our darling daughters safe at home.) Jack's hair was tightly braided where Alexis's was loose, and her hands were gloved where Alexis's were bare. But those hands were joined as tightly together as any lover's knot had ever been, and they walked in smooth, matched steps, never turning their ankles, never forcing the other to rush.

Occasionally, Jack would stop, produce a pair of bone-handled scissors from her pocket, and snip off a piece of some bush or weed. Alexis always stopped and watched indulgently as Jack made the vegetation vanish into her basket.

When they resumed, she said lightly, teasing, "You can touch every filthy plant in the world, but you can't touch me without a bucket of boiling water on hand?"

"I don't touch them," said Jack. "My scissors touch them, and my gloves touch them, but *I* don't touch them. I don't touch much of anything."

"I wish you could."

"So do I," said Jack, and smiled, a wry twist of a thing. "Sometimes I think about what my mother would say if she could see me now. She was the one who first told me that I should be afraid of getting dirty."

"My mother told me the same thing," said Alexis.

"Your mother is a reasonable terror of a woman who frightens me more than all the vampires in all the castles in the world, but she has nothing on my mother when there was a chance one of the neighbors might see me with dirt on my dress," said Jack darkly. "I learned to be afraid of dirt before I learned how to spell my own name."

"I can't imagine you in a dress," said Alexis. "You'd look . . ." She stopped herself, but it was too late: the damage was done.

"Like my sister, yes," said Jack. "We would be two peas in a terrible pod. I don't think I'd make a good vampire, though. They never seem to have a napkin on hand when the spurting starts." She shuddered theatrically. "Can you imagine me covered in all that *mess?* And they haven't reflections. I'd be unable to tell whether I'd wiped my face clean. The only solution would be dipping myself nightly in bleach."

"Hard on the hair," said Alexis.

"Hard on the heart," said Jack. She gave Alexis's fingers a squeeze. "I am what I am, and there's much about me that won't be changed with any amount of wishing or wanting. I'm sorry for that. I'd trade a great deal to share an afternoon in the hay with you, dust in the air and sweat on our skins and neither of us caring. But I'm afraid the experience would drive me mad. I am a creature of sterile environments. It's too late for me to change."

"You say that, and yet I've seen you leap into an open grave like it was nothing."

142

"Only with the proper footwear, I assure you."

Alexis laughed and stepped a little closer to Jack, hugging her arm as they walked toward the looming wall of the village. She rested her head against Jack's shoulder. Jack inhaled, breathing in the salty smell of her lover's hair, and thought that there was something to be said for worlds of blood and moonlight, where the only threat more terrible than the things that dwelt in the sea were the things that lived on the shore. Beauty was all the brighter against a background of briars.

The walk was too short, or maybe their legs had just become too long: both of them were still so haunted by the ghosts of childhood that they had yet to learn the fine art of dawdling, of stretching things out until they lasted as long as they would ask them to. In what seemed like no time at all, they were standing in front of the great wall.

Alexis let go of Jack's hand. Cupping her hands around her mouth, she called, "Alexis Chopper, returning home," to the sentry.

"Jacqueline Wolcott, apprentice to Dr. Bleak, escorting Miss Chopper and purchasing supplies," called Jack. Residents always spoke first—to give them the opportunity to scream for help if they felt that it was needed, she supposed. The "help" would probably take the form of scalding oil, or possibly a rain of arrows, but at least the residents would die knowing that they'd protected the rest of the village.

It was fascinating, how frightened people who lived in a vampire's backyard could be of the rest of the world. Just because something was unfamiliar, that didn't mean it had sharper teeth or crueler claws than the monster they already knew. But Dr. Bleak said that conducting psychological experiments on the neighbors never ended well, and he was in charge, so Jack kept her thoughts to herself.

"Watch the gate!" called the sentry. There was a lot of shouting and creaking of wood, and then the gate swung open, heavy and slow and supposedly secure.

Alexis, who had been born behind that gate, knowing that the Master watched her every step, walked through serenely. The fact that she was willingly strolling into a vampire's hunting ground didn't seem to trouble her—and maybe it didn't. On the few occasions when Jack had tried to speak to her about it, she had spoken darkly of the werewolves in the mountains, of the Drowned Gods under the sea, of all the terrible dangers that the Moors had to offer. Apparently, being a prey animal living under the auspices of a predator was better.

Maybe it was. Jack had only spent a single night under the Master's roof, and while she was sometimes sad that she hadn't been able to save her sister, she was never sorry that she'd gotten out. Jill had made her own choice.

Jack chuckled to herself. Alexis glanced at her. "Something funny?"

"Everything," said Jack, as the doors swung shut behind them. She offered Alexis her hand. "Let's go see your parents."

The sun, although fading, was still in the sky; the Master was deep inside his castle, resting up for the night that was to come. Jill was not allowed in his presence for another two days. It was always like that after a feeding. He said she needed to reach a certain age before he could stop her heart in her chest, preserving it forever. He said she would be happier facing the unending night as an adult, with an adult's position and privilege.

Jill thought it was really because he was afraid. No one had ever heard of a foundling going back to their own world after their eighteenth birthday: if you came of age in the Moors, you stayed there until you died. Or undied, as the case might be. She was only sixteen. She still had two years to wait, two years of him leaving her alone for three days every two weeks, two years of walking the battlements alone, feeling the cruel kiss of the sun on her skin. The Master insisted. He wanted the people to grow used to her, and he wanted her to fully accept what she was giving up.

Nonsense. It was all nonsense. As if anyone could be offered an eternity of privilege and power and refuse it on a whim. Anyone who walked away from the Master would have to be a fool, or worse—

There was a flicker of motion down in the square. Two people had entered via the mountainside gate. The fat girl from the inn, and a skinny figure in a black vest. Light glinted off Jack's glasses when she turned her head. Jill felt her hated, hated heart clench in her chest. Her sister, here.

This could not be allowed to stand.

9 SOMEONE'S COMING TO DINNER

The inn owned by Alexis's parents was small and cozy and reasonably clean, as such things went. Jack could be in it for hours before she started wanting to scratch her own skin off, which was remarkable for anyplace outside of the lab.

(Alexis had remarked once, after a particularly tense visit, that it was odd how Jack could handle working in the garden for Dr. Bleak, but not the idea of sitting on a seat that another human had used without first scrubbing it to a mirror sheen. Jack had attempted, not very well, to explain that dirt was dirt; dirt was capable of being clean, if it was in its native environment. It was the mixture of dirt and other things—like sweat and skin and the humors of the human body—that became a problem. It was the recipe, not the ingredients.)

Alexis's mother looked like her, but older, and when she smiled, it was like someone had lit a jack-o'-lantern fire in the space behind her eyes. Jack thought she could endure any amount of dirt for the warmth of Ms. Chopper's smile. She had searched her memory over and over again, and never found anything that even implied her own mother had been capable of such a smile.

Alexis's father had been a woodcutter before he'd settled into the innkeeper's life: hence the family name and the axe that hung above the fire. He was a mountain of a man, and Jack thought he might be the only human in the Moors who would stand a chance against Dr. Bleak in a physical contest. (The werewolves would win, no contest. Fortunately, werewolves were less interested in wrestling and axe-hurling than they were in mauling people and fetching sticks.)

As always at the Sign of the Hind and Hare, the food was simple and plentiful, and reminded Jack uncomfortably of the rabbit and root vegetables she'd eaten on her one night with the Master. He took what he wanted from the village stores for the people who lived under his roof: she had no doubt that her very first meal had been prepared by Ms. Chopper's loving hand. Maybe Alexis had eaten the same thing that night. Maybe they had started her tenure in the Moors by sharing a meal, all unaware of what lay ahead of them.

She hoped so. It made the bread taste better, and the milk seem sweeter, to think they'd been eating together for as long as that.

Ms. Chopper was passing the potatoes around the table one more time when the kitchen door blew open, shuddering in its frame like it had been caught in a heavy wind. Alexis jumped.

Mr. Chopper tensed, hand going to his side like he expected to find his axe hanging there, ready to be swung. Ms. Chopper froze, her hands clenching around the edges of her tray.

Jack sat quietly, her eyes on her food, trying to look as if she thought stewed mushrooms and roast rabbit was the most fascinating thing in the entire world.

"You could at least say hello, *sister,*" hissed Jill, and her voice was poisonously sweet, like something that had been allowed to sit too long in the sun and had spoiled from the heat.

"Oh, I'm sorry." Jack raised her head, reaching up to adjust her glasses as she did. "I thought it was a stray dog knocking the door open. Where I come from, people knock."

"You come from the same place I do," said Jill.

"Yes, and people knocked."

Jill glared at her. Jack looked impassively back. Their faces were identical: there was no denying that. All the time in the world wouldn't change the shape of their lips or the angle of their eyes. They could dye their hair, style themselves entirely differently, but they would always be cast from the same mold. But that was where the resemblance ended.

Jill was dressed in a gown of purple so pale that it might as well have been white, if not set against the pallor of her skin and the icy blonde of her hair. It was cut straight across her chest in a style that was modest now, although it wouldn't be for much longer; it was a little girl's dress, and she, like Jack, was well on her way to womanhood. Her skirt was long enough to trail on the ground. The bottom six inches or so were gray with dirt. Jack shuddered slightly, hoping her sister wouldn't see.

No such luck. While Jack had been living in a windmill, learning the secrets of science and how to raise the dead, Jill had been living in a castle, learning the secrets of survival and how to serve the dead. Her eyes saw all. Slowly, she smiled.

"Aw, I'm sorry, sister," she said. "Am I dirty? Does that bother you, that I'm a dirty girl? The Master doesn't mind if I spoil my dresses. I can always get another."

"How nice for you," said Jack, through gritted teeth. "Why are you here?"

"I saw you come through the gates. I thought surely you *must* be coming up to the castle to see me, since I'm your sister, after all, and it's been so long since you last came to visit. Imagine my surprise when you followed your little fat girl to the inn to stuff your face." Jill's nose wrinkled. "Really, it's bestial. Is this the way you want to spend your youth? With pigs and peasants?"

Jack started to stand. Alexis grabbed her wrist, pulling her back down.

"It's not worth it," she said, voice low. "Please, it's not worth it."

Jill laughed. "See? Everyone here knows their place except for you. Is it because you're jealous? Because you could have had what I have, and you didn't move fast enough? Or is it because you miss me?"

"I never knew my sister well enough to miss her, and with the way you behave, I'm not sure I'd want you for my sister," said Jack. "As for having what you have . . . you have a dress that shows every speck of dust that lands on it. You have hands so pale that they can never look clean. I don't want what you have. What you have is terrible. Leave me alone."

"Is that any way to talk to your family? Blood of your blood?"

Jack sneered. "Last time I checked, you were planning to get rid of your blood as soon as the Master was willing to take it. Or did you change your mind? Are you going to stick around and try living for a little while? I recommend it. Maybe get some more sun. You're clearly vitamin D–deficient."

"Jack, please," whispered Alexis.

Jill was still smiling. Jack went cold.

The Sign of the Hind and Hare was the only inn the village had. That didn't make it indispensable. If something should happen to it—if it burned to the ground in the middle of the night, say, or if its owners were found with all the blood drained from their bodies—well, that would just be too bad. Another inn would open before the next full moon, equipped with a new family, eager to serve without breaking the rules.

Like everyone who lived under the grace of the Master, the Choppers obeyed his rules. They did as they were told. They went where they were bid. And they didn't fight, ever, not with him, and not with the girl he'd chosen as his heir.

Jack swallowed. Jack smoothed her vest with the heels of her gloved hands and stood, leaving her plate behind. Alexis let go of her arm. The moment of absence, when the pressure of Alexis's hand was first removed, was somehow worse than the surrender.

"I'm . . . so sorry, Jillian," said Jack, in a careful, measured voice. "I was hungry. You know how cranky I get when I'm hungry."

Jill giggled. "You're the *worst* when you haven't eaten. So did you come to visit me, really?"

"Yes. Absolutely." Jack didn't need to turn to know that Alexis was trembling, or that her parents were fighting not to rush to her. They hadn't been expecting her to bring danger to their door. They should have been. They should have known. *She* should have known. She'd been a fool, and now they were paying the price. "Dr. Bleak expects me back by midnight, but I have shopping to do in the square before then. Would you like to come with me? I think I have enough coin that I could buy you something nice. Candied ginger, or a ribbon for your hair."

Jill's gaze sharpened. "If you'd really come to see me, you'd know whether you had enough coin to get me a present."

"Dr. Bleak controls the money. I'm just his apprentice." Jack spread her hands, trying to look contrite without seeming overly eager. Jill seemed to believe her—or maybe Jill just didn't care, as long as she got her own way in the end. *We're strangers now,* she thought, and mourned. "I'm learning a lot, but that doesn't mean he trusts me with more than he has to."

"The Master trusts me with *everything,*" said Jill, and skipped—skipped!—across the room to slide her arm through Jack's. "I suppose we can shop before you buy me a present. If Dr. Bleak cast you out, you'd have to live in the barn with the pigs, and you'd be filthy all the time. That would be awful, wouldn't it?"

Jack, who already felt like she needed a bath from just that short contact with her sister, suppressed a shudder. "Awful," she agreed, and grabbed her basket, and let Jill lead her out into the night.

The door slammed shut behind them. Ms. Chopper dropped the tray of potatoes in her hurry to fling her arms around her daughter, and the three of them huddled together, shaking and crying, and suddenly all too aware of the dark outside.

· · ·

Jill stepped lightly, like she was dancing her way across the muddy cobblestones in the village square. She never stopped talking, words spilling over each other like eager puppies as she recounted everything that had happened to her in the months since she'd last seen her sister. Jack realized, with a dull, distant sort of guilt, that Jill was lonely: she might have servants in that great pile of a castle, and she might have the love, or at least the fondness, of her Master, but she didn't have *friends*.

(That was probably a good thing. Jack could remember Dr. Bleak returning from trips to the village shortly after she'd gone to live with him, a dire expression on his face and his big black medical bag in his hands. There had been deaths among the village children. That was all he'd been willing to tell her, when she pressed. It hadn't been until years later, when Alexis started coming around, that she'd learned that all the children who'd died had been seen playing with Jill around the fountain. The Master was a jealous man. He didn't want her to have anything in her life except for him, and he was happy to do whatever he deemed necessary to make sure that he remained the center of her world. Friends were a nuisance to be dealt with. Friends were expendable.)

Jack was accustomed to doing her shopping alone, or in the company of Dr. Bleak. It was surprising how often people forgot that Jill was her sister, or felt no need to guard their tongues in her presence. She was used to jokes and gossip, and even the occasional sly barb about the Master's policies.

As she walked through the shops on Jill's arm, the real surprise was the silence. People who knew her as Dr. Bleak's apprentice went quiet when she approached side by side with the Master's daughter, and some of them looked at her face like she was a riddle that had just been unexpectedly solved. Jack had to fight not to grimace. It would take her months, maybe years, to rebuild the ground she was losing with every person who saw her in Jill's company. Suddenly, she was the enemy again. It was not a comfortable prospect.

Several of the merchants tried to give her deeper discounts than they usually did, or could afford. When possible, she paid the normal amount anyway, shaking her head to silence them. Unfortunately, if Jill caught her, she would snatch the coins from the merchant's hand, rolling her eyes.

"We only *pay* as a courtesy," she would say. "We *pay* as a symbol, to show that we're part of this village, not just the beating heart that sustains it in a world of wolves. If they want to make the symbol even more symbolic, you're to let them. You promised me a present."

"Yes, sister," Jack would reply, and on they would go to the next merchant, while the hole in the pit of her stomach got bigger and bigger, until it felt like it was going to swallow the entire world.

She'd have to tell Dr. Bleak about this. If she didn't, the villagers would, the next time he came for supplies or to check on someone's ailing mother. They would talk about his apprentice and the Master's daughter walking arm in arm, and he would wonder why she'd hid it from him, and everything would be ruined. Even more ruined than it already was.

The basket over her arm was heavy with the things she'd been sent to buy, and with an occasional extra that Jill had picked up and simply placed among everything else. A jug of heavy cream; a jar of honey. Luxuries that were nice, in their way, but which had never been considered necessary in the windmill up on the hill. Finally, it was time for Jill to choose her gift.

The stallholder, a slender village maiden who shook and shivered like a reed dancing in the wind, stood with her hands clasped tight against her apron, like by refusing to let them flutter, she could somehow conceal the rest of her anxiety. And maybe she could: Jill didn't appear to notice. She was busy running her fingers through the ribbons, cooing and twittering about the feel of the fabric against her skin.

Jack tried to make eye contact with the stallholder. She looked away, refusing to let Jack look into her eyes. Jack felt the hole in her stomach grow greater still. Most of the villagers were superstitious, if it could be called that when the vampire was *right there,* when there were werewolves in the mountains and terrible things with tentacles in the sea. They knew that the Master could influence their minds by meeting their eyes. None of them had looked directly at Jill without being ordered to in years, even though she wouldn't have her own power over the human heart until she was transformed. Now, it seemed, some of that superstition was transferring to Jack.

"Do you like this one?" asked Jill, holding up a length of shimmering gray silk that looked like it had been sliced out of the mist on the moor. "I have a dress it would look perfect with."

"It's beautiful," said Jack. "You should get that one."

Jill pouted prettily. "But there are so *many* of them," she protested. "I haven't seen more than half."

"I know," said Jack, trying to sound soothing, or at least, trying not to sound frustrated. "Dr. Bleak expects me back by midnight, remember? I can't disobey my master any more than you can disobey yours."

It was a calculated risk. Jill knew what it was to

158

be obedient, to bend her desires to another's. She also had a tendency to fly into a towering rage at the slightest implication that *her* Master was not the only master in the Moors, as if having a capital letter on his name somehow gave him a monopoly on shouting orders.

Jill wound the ribbon around her finger and said, "The Master would be happy to have you still, if you wanted to come home. You're very unsuitable now, you know. You'd have to be reeducated. I'd have to teach you how to be a *lady*. But you could come home."

The thought of calling the castle "home" was enough to make Jack woozy with terror. She damped it down and shook her head, saying, "I appreciate the offer. I have work to do with Dr. Bleak. I *like* what we do together. I like what I'm learning." An old memory stirred, of her mother in a pink pantsuit, telling her how to refuse an invitation. "Thank you so much for thinking of me."

Jill sighed. "You'll come home one day," she said, and grabbed a fistful of ribbons, so many of them that they trailed between her fingers like a rainbow of worms. "I'll take these," she informed the stallholder. "My sister will pay you." Then she was gone, turning on her heel and flouncing back toward the castle gates. Ribbons fell unnoticed from her fist as she walked, leaving a trail behind her in the dust.

Jack turned back to the stallholder, reaching for the coins at the bottom of her basket. "I'm so sorry," she said, voice pitched low and urgent. "I didn't mean to bring her to you. She forced my hand. I may not have enough to pay you, but I promise, I'll return with the rest, only tell me what I owe."

"Nothing," said the stallholder. She still wasn't looking at Jack.

"But—"

"I said, nothing." The stallholder moved to start smoothing the remaining ribbons, trying to restore order to the chaos Jill had made. "She never pays anyway. The Master will send someone with gold, will overpay for the next dress he orders in her name. She didn't threaten me this time. She didn't show me her teeth or ask if I wanted to look at the skin under her choker. You made her better, not worse."

"I'm so sorry."

"Leave." The stallholder finally looked up, finally focused on Jack. When she spoke again, her voice was so soft that it was barely audible. "Everyone knows that children who talk to the Master's daughter disappear, because he can't stand to share her. But not you. Because even though you're not his child, you're still her sister, and *she* gets jealous of the people who talk to *you*. Get away from me before she decides you're my friend."

Jack took a step backward. The stallholder went

back to sorting through her ribbons, expression grim. She did not speak again, and so Jack turned and walked through the silent village. The sun was down. The huge red moon hung ominously close to the horizon, like it might descend and begin crushing everything in its path.

The door of the inn was closed. A single candle burned in the window. Jack looked at it and kept on walking, out of the village, through the gates, and onto the wild and lonely moor.

The light in the windmill window made it seem more like a lighthouse, something perfect and pure, calling the lost souls home. Jack started to walk a little faster when she realized that she was almost home. That wasn't enough. She broke into a run, and would have slammed straight into the door if Dr. Bleak hadn't opened it a split second before she could. She ran into the hard flesh of his midsection instead, the rough leather of his apron grinding against her cheek.

She dropped the basket, scattering supplies and her small remaining store of coins at her feet.

"Jack, what's wrong?" asked Dr. Bleak, and his voice was a rope thrown to a drowning girl, his voice was the solid foundation of her world, and she clung to him, pressing her face against his chest, for once not caring about the dirt, and cried and cried, under the eye of the unforgiving moon.

PART IV

JILL AND JACK
WILL NOT COME BACK

10 AND FROM HER GRAVE, A RED, RED ROSE . . .

Time passed. Jack stayed away from the village, electing to do extra chores at home rather than accompanying Dr. Bleak to town on shopping trips. She began to make plans for the future, for the time when she would have her own garden, her own windmill, and be able to provide for a household of her own.

Alexis continued to visit, cautiously at first, and then more and more brazenly as nothing terrible happened to her family.

Jill walked the battlements, and counted down the days until their eighteenth birthday. She was nestled snug in her bed, dreaming of rivers of beautiful red, when sunlight flooded the room and slapped her out of sleep. She sat bolt upright, shocked and bewildered, and blinked against the terrible brightness.

"Miss," said Mary, voice polite, deferential. She had been using that tone with Jill for two years, since the day Jill had thrown a fit and demanded she be spoken to with respect, lest

Mary find herself thrown over the battlements. "The Master requested I wake you."

"Why?" demanded Jill. She dug at her eyes with the heels of her hands, rubbing until the sting of the sunlight faded. When she lowered her hands, blinking rapidly, she realized that Mary was holding a large vase filled with red, red roses. Jill's eyes widened. She reached out her hands, making small wanting motions.

"Give them to me," said Jill.

"Yes, miss." Mary did not hand the vase to Jill. Rather, she walked a few steps along the length of the bed and set them on the table next to the headboard, where Jill could breathe in their fragrance and admire their beauty without pricking herself on the thorns. If she were responsible for the Master's precious girl bleeding when he was not in the room, her head would be the one hitting the floor.

"From the Master?" demanded Jill.

"Yes, miss."

"They're *beautiful.*" Jill's expression went soft, her eyes growing wet with grateful tears. "Do you see how beautiful they are? He loves me so much. He's so good to me."

"Yes, miss," said Mary, who was well acquainted with the shape of a vampire's love. She thought sometimes that Jill had utterly forgotten that she had been a foundling too, long ago; that Jill was not the first girl to wear a pale dress and a choker around her throat.

"Did he tell you why?" Jill turned a hopeful face toward Mary. "Is he coming to see me today? I know it's only been two days, but—"

"Do you really not know, miss?" Of course she didn't. Vampires cared about time only as it impacted other people, and Jill, while still human, was already thinking like a vampire. Mary forced herself to smile. "Today is the fifth anniversary of your arrival in the Moors."

Jill's eyes widened. "I'm seventeen?"

"Yes, miss." Time in the Moors was not precisely like time in the world Jack and Jill had originally come from: it followed a different set of natural rules and did not map precisely to any other calendar. But a year was a year. Even if their precise birthday was impossible to mark, the date of their arrival was clear.

Jill tumbled out of bed in an avalanche of blankets and fluffy nightgown. "I was almost twelve and a half when we arrived here," she said excitedly, starting to shovel her covers back onto the mattress. "That makes me practically eighteen. Does he want me? Tonight? Is it finally time?"

"Practically eighteen is not the same as actually eighteen, miss," said Mary, fighting to keep the precise balance of kindness and deference she needed when speaking to Jill. "He knew you would ask about this. He said to tell you that because we do not know your precise birthday, he will err on the side of caution; things will continue as they are until the Drowned Abbey rings the bells for the change of seasons."

"But that's *forever!*" protested Jill. "Why so long? I've done nothing wrong! I've been so good! Everything he's asked me to be, I've become!" She dropped her armload of pillows and straightened, waving her hands to indicate the elegant lace of her nightgown, the carefully arrayed curl of her hair. She had long since mastered the art of sleeping motionlessly, so as to rise perfectly coifed and ready to face whatever the night might hold.

"Everything except an adult," said Mary gently. "The door could still open for you. The world of your birth could still pull you back."

"That's a bedtime story to frighten children," snapped Jill. "Doors don't come back when they're not wanted."

"You knew what a vampire was when you came here," said Mary. "Didn't you wonder why that was? The rules we have exist because mistakes have been made in the past. Things have gone wrong." Newly made vampires, things of anger and appetite, stumbling through magical doors and back into worlds that had no defenses against them . . .

Mary suppressed the urge to shiver. The Moors

knew how to live with vampires. The Moors were equipped to survive alongside their own monsters.

"Had you gone to the mountains and the care of the werewolf lord, he would tell you the same," she said. "Or down to the sea. The Drowned Gods change no one young enough to go back to where they came from. We must be careful, lest we attract the attention of whatever force creates the doors. If they stopped, the Moors would be lost."

"The Moon makes the doors," said Jill in a waspish tone. "Everyone knows that."

"There are other theories."

"Those theories are wrong." Jill glared at her. "The door we used said 'Be Sure' on it, and I'm sure. I'm sure I want to be a vampire. I want to be strong and beautiful and *forever*. I want to know that no one can ever, ever take all this away from me. Why can't I have that?"

"You will," said Mary. "When the bells of the Drowned Abbey ring, you will. The Master will take you to the highest tower, and he'll make you ruthless, and he'll make you swift, and most of all, he'll make you his. But you must wait for the bells to ring, miss, you must. I know it's difficult. I know you don't want to wait. But—"

"What do *you* know, Mary?" snapped Jill. "You were a foundling. This could have been yours. You refused him. Why?"

"Because I didn't want to be ruthless, miss." It had all seemed like a game at first, her and the vampire in the high castle, him offering her whatever she wanted, while she laughed and refused everything but what she needed. It had seemed like a *game*.

And then he had asked to be her new father, and asked her to be his child, to rule alongside him forever in fury and in blood.

And then he had raged at her refusal. Her friends from the village kept disappearing, and at first that had seemed like a game too, a vast conspiracy of hide-and-seek . . . until the day he'd dragged little Bela in front of her and said "This is what becomes of those who oppose me," and ripped the boy's throat out with his teeth. Sometimes Mary thought she could still feel the blood on her face.

But Jill had never seen that side of him. Jill had been his precious little princess from the start. Jill walked on clouds and dreamt of vampirism like it was a wonderful game, still a wonderful game, and there was no way Mary could convince her otherwise.

Jill's face hardened. "I can be ruthless," she said. "I'll show him that I can be ruthless, and then he'll see that we don't have to wait. I can be his daughter right now."

"Yes, miss," said Mary. "Do you want breakfast?"

"Don't be stupid," said Jill, which meant "yes." In that regard, at least, the girl was already a vampire: she was always hungry.

"Thank you, miss," said Mary, and made her exit as quickly and gracefully as possible.

Jill watched her go, face still hard. Once she was sure the other woman would not be coming back she turned and walked to her wardrobe, pulling it open to reveal a rainbow of pastel dresses. She selected the palest of them, a cream silk gown that brought out the gold in her hair and the ivory in her skin. It was the next best thing to white, to a wedding gown. She would show him that she didn't need to wait.

She would show him that she already understood what it was to be ruthless.

Today was the anniversary of their arrival. The Master would no doubt host a party in her honor when the sun went down, something decadent and grand. He might even invite the other vampires to come and coo over his protégée, how far she'd come, how beautiful she was. Yes: it would be a lovely affair, and the only way it could be better was if it ended with her glorious demise and even more glorious rebirth.

Waiting was pointless. Even if a door opened, she wouldn't go through it. She would never leave her beloved Master like that. All she needed to do was prove to him that she was serious, that she was ruthless enough to be his child, and everything would be perfect.

If there was to be a party in her honor, something glorious and befitting a vampire's child, that dreadful Dr. Bleak would be doing something for Jack as well. He had to. Everyone knew that being a mad scientist's apprentice wasn't as good as being the Master's daughter, and that meant that Dr. Bleak couldn't afford to miss any opportunity to bind Jack's loyalty more tightly to him. There would be a party.

And if there was a party, Alexis would be attending.

Jack's unnatural fondness for the innkeeper's daughter had not faded with time; if anything, it had grown more intense. Jill had seen them together many times. Jack laughed when she was with Alexis. *Laughed,* like she wasn't making them both look bad by wandering around the Moors in ugly vests and cravats, acting like a lady had any place in a nasty old mad scientist's lab. It wasn't right. It wasn't proper.

Jill could fix everything. She could set her sister on the right path and show the Master that she was ruthless enough to be his child in truth, not just in name. One single act would make it all better.

She wrinkled her nose in distaste before taking a heavy brown cloak down from its peg inside the wardrobe and fastening it over her beautiful gown. She hated dull, ordinary colors, but it was necessary. She knew how much she stood out when she didn't take steps to hide herself.

Mary was still downstairs, seeing to breakfast. Jill slipped through the secret door on the landing—every good castle had secret doors—and started down the stairs. She had made this walk so many times that she could do it with her eyes closed, and so she let her mind drift, thinking about how wonderful it would be when the Master took her in his arms and showed her all the mysteries that death had to offer.

Soon. So soon.

She emerged from a small door at the base of the castle wall, secluded and mostly concealed by a fold in the architecture. Pulling her hood up over her head, she walked into the village, keeping her cloak closed, attracting no attention to herself. Mysterious cloaked figures were a common enough occurrence in the Moors that no one gave her a second look. It was best not to interfere with people who might be carrying secret messages for the Master, or looking for sacrifices to carry back to the Drowned Gods.

The village looked different by day. Smaller, meaner, *filthier*. Jill walked through the streets, imagining the way people would shy away if they knew who she was. It almost made up for the dirt that stained her hem, turning it from cream to muddy brown. She didn't mind mess the way Jack did, but it wasn't *elegant*. Hard to strike a terrifying figure when it looked as if she'd forgotten to do the laundry.

The villagers were surprisingly noisy when not watching their tongues in the presence of the Master's daughter. People laughed and shouted to one another, bargaining, talking about the harvest. Jill frowned under the safety of her hood. They sounded *happy*. But they lived short, brutish lives, protected only by the grace of the Master. They wallowed in dirt and worked their fingers to the bone just to keep a roof over their heads. How could they be *happy?*

It was a train of thought that might have led her to some unpleasant conclusions had it been allowed to continue; this story might have ended differently. A single revelation does not change a life. It is a start. But alas, the inn door opened; the innkeeper's daughter emerged, dressed in what passed among the villagers for finery. Her dress was green, her bodice was blue, and her skirts were hiked daringly high enough to show her ankles. There was a basket over one arm, laden with bread and wine and fresh-picked apples.

Her mother, coming to the threshold, said something. The girl laughed, and leaned in to kiss her mother's cheek. Then she turned and started for the gate, walking like she hadn't a care in the world.

On silent feet, Jill followed.

Jill rarely left the safety of the castle and

village, where the Master's word was absolute law and no one would dare to raise a hand against her. The moor outside the walls was his as well, of course, but the territories could get murky out in the open. Those who walked too carelessly were always at risk of werewolf attack, or being selected as a sacrifice for the Drowned Gods. The walk into the bracken was thus tainted with a giddy wickedness, like she was getting away with something. Surely this would prove how serious she was!

The innkeeper's daughter walked surprisingly fast. Jill stayed just far enough behind her to go unnoticed.

Alexis had grown up in the shadow of the castle, hearing the werewolves howl at night and the ringing of the bells in the Drowned Abbey. She was a survivor. But she knew that her status as one of the resurrected made her unappealing to many of the monsters she had grown up fearing, and she knew that neither gargoyles nor phantom hounds prowled during the day, and besides, she was going to see the woman she loved. She was relaxed. She was daydreaming. She was careless.

A hand touched her shoulder. Alexis stiffened and turned, preparing for the worst. She relaxed when she saw the face peeping at her from beneath the concealing hood.

"Jack," she said warmly. "I thought you had chores all morning."

Jill frowned. Alexis, finally realizing that the woman behind her wasn't wearing glasses, took a stumbling step backward.

"You're not Jack," she said. "What are you doing here?"

"Being sure," said Jill. She unfastened her cloak, letting it fall into the bracken as she drew the knife from inside her bodice, and leapt.

We will leave them there. There are some things that do not need to be seen to be understood; things that can be encompassed by a single sharp scream, and by a spray of blood painting the heather, red as roses, red as apples, red as the lips of the vampire's only child.

There is nothing here for us now.

11 ... AND FROM HIS GRAVE, A BRIAR

"She should *be* here by now," said Jack, putting aside the bone saw she had been carefully sharpening. Her eyes went to the open door, and to the moor beyond. Alexis did not appear. "I told her we were going to have supper at nightfall."

Alexis had been granted permission to stay the night at the windmill. It would have been considered improper, but with Dr. Bleak to serve as a chaperone, there was no question of her virtue being imperiled. (Not that her parents had any illusions about her virtue, or about Jack's intentions toward their daughter. Despite Alexis's status as one of the resurrected, they were both relieved to know that she had found someone who would care for her when they were gone.)

Dr. Bleak looked up from his own workbench. "Perhaps she stopped to pick flowers."

"On the moor?" Jack stood, grabbing her jacket from the back of the chair. "I'm going to go find her."

"Patience, Jack—"

"Is an essential tool of the scientific mind; raise

no corpse before its time. I know, sir. But I also know that this isn't like Alexis. She's never late." Jack looked at her mentor, expression pleading.

Dr. Bleak sighed. "Ah, for the energy of the young," he said. "Yes, you may go and find her. But be quick about it. The festivities will not begin until you finish your chores."

"Yes, sir," said Jack. She yanked on her gloves, and then she was off, running for the door and down the garden path. Dr. Bleak watched her until she had dwindled to almost nothing in the distance. Only then did he close his eyes. He had lived in the Moors for a very long time. He knew, even better than Jack did, that lateness was rarely, if ever, as innocent as it seemed.

"Let her be alive," he whispered, and recognized his words for the useless things they were as soon as he heard them. He sat still, waiting. The truth would come clear soon enough.

It was the red that caught Jack's attention first.

The Moors were far more complex than they had seemed to her on that first night, when she had been young and innocent and unaware of her own future. They were brown, yes, riddled with dead and dying vegetation. Every shade of brown that there was could be found on the Moors. They were also bright with growing green and mellow gold, and with the rainbow pops of flowers—

yellow marigold and blue heather and purple wolf's bane. Hemlock bloomed white as clouds. Foxglove spanned the spectrum of sunset. The Moors were beautiful in their own way, and if their beauty was the quiet sort that required time and introspection to be seen, well, there was nothing wrong with that. The best beauty was the sort that took some seeking.

But nothing red grew on the Moors. Not even strawberries, or poisonous mushrooms. Those were found only on the outskirts of the forest held by the werewolves, or in private gardens, like Dr. Bleak's. The Moors were neutral territory, of a sort, divided between so many monsters that they could not bear to bleed. Red was an anomaly. Red was aftermath.

Jack began to walk faster.

The closer she got, the clearer the red became. It was like it had exploded outward from a single source, shed with wanton delight by whoever held the knife. There was a body at the center of it, a softly curving body, lush of breast and generous of hip. A body . . . a body . . .

Jack stopped dead, eyes fixed not on the body but on the basket that had fallen at the very edge of the carnage. It had landed on its side. Some of the bread was splattered with blood, but the apples had already been red; there was no way of telling whether they were clean. No way in the world.

Slowly, Jack sank to her knees in the bracken, for once utterly heedless of the possibility of mud or grass stains. Her eyes bulged as she stared at the basket, never looking any further than that; never looking at the things she didn't want to see.

Red. So much red.

When she began to howl, it was the senseless keen of someone who has been pushed past their breaking point and taken refuge in the comforting caverns of their own mind. In the village, people gathered their children close, shivering, and closed the windows. In the castle, the Master stirred in his sleep, troubled for reasons he could not name.

In the windmill, Dr. Bleak rose, sorrow etched into his features, and reached for his bag. Things from here would continue as they would. It was too late to control or prevent them. All he could do was hope that they'd survive.

Jack was still on her knees in the bracken when Dr. Bleak walked up behind her, his boots crunching dry stalks underfoot. He made no effort to soften the sound of his footsteps; he wanted her to hear him coming.

She didn't react. Her eyes were fixed on the apples. So red. So red.

"The blood should get darker as it dries," she said, voice dull. "I'll be able to tell which ones are dirty, then. I'll be able to tell which ones can be saved."

"I'm sorry, Jack," said Dr. Bleak softly. He didn't share her squeamishness—understandable, given her youth, and how much she had cared for Alexis. He allowed his eyes to travel the length of the dead girl's body, noting the deep cuts, the blood loss, the places where it looked as if the flesh had been roughly hacked away.

Second resurrections were always difficult, even when the body was in perfect condition. Alexis . . . She was so damaged that he wasn't sure he could succeed, or that she would still be herself if he did. Sometimes, the twice-dead came back wrong, unstoppable monstrosities of science.

"I will, if you ask me to," he said abruptly. "You know I will. But I will expect you to help me if it goes wrong."

Jack raised her head, slowly turning to look at her mentor. "I don't care if it goes wrong," she said. "I just . . . It can't end this way."

"Then follow the blood, Jack. If a beast has taken her heart, I'll want it intact. The more of the original flesh we have to work with, the higher our chances will be of bringing her back whole." That was true, but it was also a convenient distraction. Dr. Bleak knew enough about bodies to know that Alexis would reveal more injuries when she was lifted. The dead always did. If he could spare Jack the sight . . .

Sparing Jack had never been his goal. If the

girl was to survive in the Moors, she needed to understand the world into which she had fallen. But there was preparing her for the future, and then there was being cruel. He was perfectly happy to do the former. He would never do the latter. Not if he could help it.

"Yes, sir," said Jack, and staggered to her feet, beginning to follow the drips and drops of blood across the open ground. She had spent so many years looking for the slightest hint of a mess that she had absolutely no trouble following a blood trail. She was so focused on her feet that she didn't hear Dr. Bleak grunt as he hoisted Alexis's body up and onto his shoulders, turning to carry her back toward the distant shadow of the windmill.

Jack walked, on and on, until she reached the village wall. The gate was open. The gate was often open during the high part of the day. The sound of raised voices from inside was more unusual. It sounded like people were shouting.

She stepped through the gate. The noise took on form, meaning:

"Beast!"

"Monster! *Monster!*"

"Kill the witch!"

Jack stopped where she was, frowning as she tried to make sense of the scene. What looked like half the village was standing in the square, fists raised in anger. Some of them held knives or pitchforks; one enterprising soul had even stopped to find himself a torch. She would have admired the can-do spirit, if not for the figure at the center of their mob:

Jill, a confused expression on her face, blood gluing her gauzy dress to her body, so that she looked like she had just gone for a swim. Her arms were red to the elbow; her hands were terrors, slathered so thickly in red that it was as if they were gloved.

Ms. Chopper pushed her way through the throng, shrieking, *"Demon!"* before she flung an egg at Jill. It hit the front of her dress and burst, adding a smear of yellow to the red.

Jill's eyes widened. "You can't do that," she said, in a surprisingly childish voice. "I'm the Master's daughter. You can't do that to me. It's not *allowed*."

"You're not his daughter yet, you foolish girl," snapped a new voice—a familiar one. Both Jack and Jill turned in unconscious unison to see Mary standing at the edge of the crowd, blocking Jill from the castle. "I told you to be patient. I told you that your time would come. You just had to rush things, didn't you? I told him he did you no favors by cosseting you."

"You told me to be ruthless!" protested Jill, balling her bloody hands into fists. "You said that he needed me to be ruthless!"

"The Master feeds from the village, but he

protects them as well," said Mary coldly. "You have killed without his permission and without his blessing, and you are no vampire; you had no right." She lifted her chin slightly, shifting her attention to the crowd. "The Master has revoked the protection of his household. Do with her as you will."

A low, dangerous rumble spread through the crowd. It was the sound a beast made immediately before it attacked.

Perhaps Jack could have been forgiven if she had turned her back on her bewildered sister, still dressed in her lover's blood; if she had walked away. These were extraordinary circumstances, after all, and while Jack was an extraordinary girl, she was only seventeen. It would have been understandable of her to hold a grudge, even if she might have regretted it later.

She looked at Jill and remembered a twelve-year-old in blue jeans, short hair spiking up at the back, trying to talk her into having an adventure. She remembered how afraid she'd been to leave her sister behind, even if it had meant saving them both. She remembered Gemma Lou, when they were small—so small!—telling them to look out for each other, even when they were angry, because family was a thing that could never be replaced once it was thrown away.

She remembered loving her sister, once, a long, long time ago.

The crowd had been watching Jill for signs that she was preparing to run away. They hadn't been expecting Jack to push her way into the center of their ring, grab Jill's hand, and run. Surprise was enough to get the two girls to the edge of the crowd, Jack hauling her sister in her wake, struggling not to let the blood make her lose her grip. Jill was strangely pliant, not resisting Jack's efforts to pull her along. It was like she was in shock.

Becoming a murderer and getting disowned in the same day will do that, thought Jack dizzily, and kept on running, even as the first sounds of pursuit began behind them. All that mattered now was getting away. Everything else could happen later.

12 EVERYTHING YOU NEVER WANTED

See them now, two girls—almost women, but still not quite, not quite—running hand in hand across the vast and unforgiving moor. One wears a skirt that tangles and tears in the bracken. The other wears trousers, sturdy shoes, and gloves to protect her from the world around her. Both of them run like their lives depend on it.

Behind them, a river of anger, split into individual human bodies, running with the unstoppable fury of the crowd. More torches have been found and lit; more pitchforks have been liberated. In a place like this, under a sky like this, torches and pitchforks are the native trappings of the enraged. They appear without being asked for, and the more there are, the deeper the danger.

The crowd glitters like a starry sky with the individual flames of their ire. The danger is very real.

Jack runs and Jill follows. Both of them are weeping, the one for her lover blooming red as a rose in the empty moorland, the other for her adoptive father, who should have been so proud of her and has instead cast her aside. If our sympathy is more for the first of them, well, we are only human; we can only look on the scene with human eyes, and judge in our own ways.

They run, and the crowd pursues, and the rising moon observes, for the tale is almost ending.

Dr. Bleak covered Alexis with an oiled tarp when he heard footsteps pounding up the garden path. He turned, expecting to see Jack, and went still when he saw not only his apprentice but her bloody sister. Behind them, the furious body of the mob was gaining ground, outlined by the glow from their torches.

"Jack," he said. "What . . . ?"

"The Master revoked his protection when the villagers saw what she'd done to Alexis," said Jack, still running, pulling Jill into the windmill. Her voice was clear and cold: if he hadn't known her so well, he might not even have realized how badly it was shaking. "They're going to kill her."

Jill gave an almighty shriek and yanked her hand out of Jack's, letting the still-slippery blood work for her. "That's not true! He loves me!" she shouted, and whirled to run.

Dr. Bleak was somehow already there, a white rag in his hand. He clapped it over her nose and mouth, holding it in place. Jill made a desperate mewling sound, like a kitten protesting bedtime, and struggled for a few seconds before her knees folded and she fell, crumpling in on herself.

"Jack, quickly," he said, slamming the door. "There isn't much time."

Obedience had been the first thing Dr. Bleak drilled into her: failure to obey could result in nasty consequences, many of which would be fatal to a child like she had been. Jack rushed to Jill's side, gathering her unconscious sister in her arms. They were the same height, but Jill felt like she weighed nothing at all, like she was nothing but dust and down.

"We have to hide her," Jack said.

"Hiding her isn't good enough," Dr. Bleak replied. He grabbed a small machine from his workbench and moved toward the windmill's back door. "You've been an excellent apprentice, Jack. Quick-fingered, sharp-witted—you were everything I could have asked for. I'm sorry this has happened."

"What do you mean, sir?" Jack's stomach clenched in on itself. She was holding her sleeping sister, covered in the blood of her dead girlfriend, and the village was marching on the windmill with torches and pitchforks. She would have said this night couldn't get any worse. Suddenly, she was terribly sure that it could.

I've seen this movie before, she thought, almost nonsensically. *But we're not the ones who made the monster. The Master did that. We're just the ones who loved her.*

Only they weren't even that, were they? Dr. Bleak would have saved Jill instead of Jack, at the beginning, because he'd seen Jack as a more logical choice for a vampire lord. That didn't mean he'd known her or cared about her. Time is the alchemy that turns compassion into love, and Jill and Dr. Bleak had never had any time. If anyone in this room loved Jill, it was Jack, and the worst of it was, she wouldn't even have had that much if it hadn't been for Alexis. Their parents had never taught them how to love each other. Any connection they'd had had been despite the adults in their lives, not because of them.

Jill had run to the Master, and while she may have been the one who'd felt deserted, she was also the one who had never looked back. She had wanted to be a vampire's child, and vampires did not love what they were compelled to share. Jack had gone with Dr. Bleak, and he had cared for her, had taken care of her and taught her, but he had never encouraged her to *love*.

That was on Alexis. Alexis, who had walked with her in the village, introducing her to people who had only been passing faces before, telling her about their lives until she could no longer fail to recognize them as people. Alexis, who had cried with her and laughed with her and felt sorry for her sister, trapped and alone in the castle. It had been Alexis who put Jill back into a human context, and it had been seeing her sister terrified and abandoned that made Jack realize she still loved her.

Without Alexis, she might have forgotten how to love. Jill would still have killed—some villager or other, someone too slow to get out of her way—but Jack would not have saved her.

The worst of it was knowing that without Alexis, whoever played her role would have been properly avenged.

"I mean they'll kill her if they find her here, and they may kill you as well; you'd offer them a rare second chance to commit the same murder." He slapped his device onto the door, embedding its pointed "feet" in the wood, and began twisting dials. "The Master had to repudiate her to keep them from marching on the castle—even vampires fear fire—but he won't forgive them for killing his daughter. He'll burn the village to the ground. It's happened before. You did well in bringing her here. The only way to save them is to save her."

"Sir, what does that have to do with—"

"The doors are the greatest scientific mystery our world has to offer," said Dr. Bleak. He grabbed a jar of captive lightning and smashed it against the doorframe. Sparks filled the air. The device whirred into sudden life, dials spinning wildly. "Did you truly think I wouldn't find a way to harness them?"

Jack's eyes went wide. "We could have gone back anytime?" she demanded, in a voice that was barely more than a squeak.

"You could have gone back," he agreed. "But you would not have been going home."

Jack looked down at her silent, bloody sister, and sighed. "No," she said. "We wouldn't have been."

"Stay away at least a year, Jack. You have to. A year is all it takes for a mob to dissipate here; grudges are counter to survival." They could hear the shouting outside now. The flames would come next. "Blood will open the door, yours or hers, as long as it's on *your* hands. Leave her behind, or kill her and bring back her body, but she can't come here as she is. Do you understand? Do *not* bring your sister back here alive."

Jack's eyes widened further, until the muscles around them ached. "You're really sending me away? But I haven't done anything wrong!"

"You've denied the mob their kill. That, here, is more than enough. Go, stay gone, and come home if you still want to. This will always, always be your home." He looked at her sadly. "I'm going to miss you, apprentice."

"Yes, sir," whispered Jack, her lower lip shaking with the effort of keeping herself from bursting into tears. This wasn't fair. This wasn't *fair*. Jill had been the one to break the rules, and now Jack was the one on the cusp of losing everything.

Dr. Bleak opened the door. What should have been a view of the back garden was instead a wooden stairway, slowly winding upward into the dark.

Jack took a deep breath. "I'll be back," she promised.

"See that you are," he said.

She stepped through the door. He closed it behind her.

13 A THOUSAND MILES OF HARDSHIP BETWEEN HERE AND HOME

Descending the stairs as a twelve-year-old had been tiring but achievable: the work of hours, the amusement of an afternoon.

Climbing the stairs as a seventeen-year-old, arms full of limp, slumbering sister, proved to be rather more difficult. Jack clumped up them methodically, trying to focus on all the repetitive, seemingly meaningless tasks Dr. Bleak had assigned her over the years. She had spent afternoons sorting frogspawn by minute gradations in color, or removing all the seeds from forest-grown strawberries, or sharpening all the thorns in a blackberry hedge. Every one of those chores had been infuriating when it was going on, but had left her better suited to her job. So: what did this leave her better suited to?

Betraying the girl who loved her, who was dead in the Moors, who might stay that way now that Dr. Bleak had no apprentice to assist him.

Carrying the sister who had cost her everything away from the damnation she had earned.

193

Giving up everything she had finally learned she wanted.

None of those were things she *wanted* to be suited to, but they were the answer all the same. Jack shook her head to dry her tears, and kept climbing.

The stairs were still old, still solid, still dusty; here and there, she thought she saw the ghosts of her own childish footprints, going down while she was coming up. It only made sense. There had been no foundlings in the Moors since she and Jill had arrived. Maybe there would be another now, since the position was no longer filled. Every breath had to be sucking in millions of dust particles. The thought was nauseating.

They were halfway up when Jill stirred, opening her eyes and staring upward at Jack in confusion. "Jack?" she squeaked.

"Can you walk?" Jack replied brusquely.

"I . . . Where are we?"

"On the stairs." Jack stopped walking and dropped Jill, unceremoniously, on her bottom. "If you can ask questions, you can walk. I'm tired of carrying you."

Jill blinked at her, eyes going wide and shocked. "The Master—"

"Isn't *here,* Jill. We're on the stairs. You remember the stairs?" Jack waved her arms, indicating everything around them. "The Moors kicked us out. We're going back."

"No! *No!*" Jill leapt to her feet, attempting to fling herself downward.

Jack was faster than she was. She hooked an arm around her sister's waist, jerking her back up and flinging her forward. *"Yes!"* she shouted.

Jill's head hit something hard. She stopped, rubbing it, and then turned, in slow confusion, to touch the air behind her. It lifted upward, like a trapdoor—like the lid of a trunk—and revealed a small, dusty room that still smelled, ever so faintly, of Gemma Lou's perfume.

"The stairs below me have gone," said Jack's voice, dull and unsurprised. "You'd best climb out before we're pushed out."

Jill climbed out. Jack followed.

The two stood there for a long moment, stepping unconsciously closer together as they looked at the room that had belonged to their first caretaker, that had once been so familiar, before both of them had changed. The trunk slammed shut. Jill gave a little shriek and dove for it, clawing it open. Jack watched almost indifferently.

Inside the trunk was a welter of old clothing and costume jewelry, the sort of things a loving grandmother would set aside for her grandchildren to amuse themselves with. No stairway. No secret door.

Jill plunged her bloody hands into the clothes, pawing them aside. Jack let her.

"It has to be here!" Jill wailed. "It *has* to be!"

It wasn't.

When Jill finally stopped digging and bowed her head to weep, Jack put a hand on her shoulder. Jill looked up, shaking, broken. She had never learned the art of thinking for herself.

I made the right choice, and I am so sorry I left you, thought Jack. Aloud, she said, "Come."

Jill stood. When Jack took her hand, she did not resist.

The door was locked. The key Jack carried in her pocket—the key she had been carrying for five long years—fit it perfectly. It turned, and the door opened, and they were, in the strictest and most academic of senses, home.

The house they had lived in for the first twelve years of their lives (not the house they had grown up in, no; they had aged there, but they had so rarely grown) was familiar and alien at the same time, like walking through a storybook. The carpet was too soft beneath feet accustomed to stone castle floors and hard-packed earth; the air smelled of sickly-sweetness, instead of fresh flowers or honest chemicals. By the time they reached the ground floor, they were walking so close together that it didn't matter if their hands never touched; they were still conjoined.

There was a light in the dining room. They followed it and found their parents sitting at the table, along with a small, impeccably groomed boy. They stopped in the doorway, both of them looking in bemusement at this small closed circle of a family.

Serena noticed them first. She shrieked, jumping from her chair. "Chester!"

Chester turned, opening his mouth to yell at the intruders. But one of the girls was covered in blood, and they both looked as if they had been crying, and something about them . . .

"Jacqueline?" he whispered. "Jillian?"

And the two girls clung to each other and wept, as outside the rain came down like a punishment, and nothing would ever be the same.

ABOUT THE AUTHOR

Seanan lives in the Pacific Northwest with her cats, a vast collection of creepy dolls and horror movies, and sufficient books to qualify her as a fire hazard.

She was the winner of the 2010 John W. Campbell Award for Best New Writer, and in 2013 she became the first person ever to appear five times on the same Hugo ballot. She doesn't sleep much, but she spends a lot of time in the corn.

O, the corn.

| Books are produced in the United States using U.S.-based materials | Books are printed using a revolutionary new process called THINKtech™ that lowers energy usage by 70% and increases overall quality | Books are durable and flexible because of Smyth-sewing | Paper is sourced using environmentally responsible foresting methods and the paper is acid-free |

Center Point Large Print
600 Brooks Road / PO Box 1
Thorndike, ME 04986-0001 USA

(207) 568-3717

US & Canada:
1 800 929-9108
www.centerpointlargeprint.com